A BET TURNED
DEADLY

A BET TURNED
DEADLY

ALICE ZOGG

This book is a work of fiction.

Published by Aventine Press
55 East Emerson St.
Chula Vista CA 91911
www.aventinepress.com

ISBN: 978-1-59330-860-5

Library of Congress Control Number: 2014912377
Library of Congress Cataloging-in-Publication Data
A Bet Turned Deadly/Alice Zogg
Printed in the United States of America

To my friend Karen Carter

CREDITS

Credit is due to my son-in-law, Sam Levering, who came to the rescue with a wealth of information regarding camping, hiking, and roughing it in the wild. Thank you, Sam, for sharing your expert knowledge. Again, Valoise Douglas came through with an excellent editing job. As always, I counted on my daughter Franziska for proofreading the manuscript; I could never do without her. My gratitude goes out to the members of the Los Angeles chapter of Sisters in Crime. Their support and friendship keeps me excited about this thing called "writing." Last but not least, I appreciate my husband, Wilfried, who is always ready to accompany me on location research; in this book, from scouting out territory in the Angeles National Forest Mountains to a day of footing it along the vast stretch of Downtown L.A.

PROLOGUE

With the US Federal Government shutdown, the Health Care reform, and the Los Angeles Dodgers' advancement to the National League Championship series dominating the news at the beginning of October, there also appeared a less prominent news headline in the local papers of Southern California. It read:

What was left of the body, recently discovered by hikers in the Angeles National Forest Mountains, is now identified as thirty-two-year-old Jacob Barrstein, manager of Jock Master Sporting Goods, who went missing while on a camping trip in these local mountains in April of this year.

Six months after his disappearance - - wild animals and natural decomposing having run their course - - Jacob's remains were identified and the case changed from a missing person's file to a full-blown police investigation.

Eight years later

CHAPTER 1

Being an author, a fiction crime writer to be exact, I was approached more than once over the last several years with a possible book deal for the real life murder in which I had been involved. Until now I declined the offers. I wanted to forget the horrible experience and I also felt responsible for my friend's death. If I had not made the damn bet in the first place, none of the events could have happened and he would still be alive. I also had qualms about making money out of the disaster. I wish it was that simple. As it stands, I cannot get the tragedy out of my mind. The killing of Jacob has even affected my writing, stifling my creativity. My psychiatrist tells me that I need to write about the incident in order to get closure. So I'll give in and put the sordid events down on paper.

All of this happened years ago, when we began to rely heavily on electronic devices but before technology was at today's advanced state. For instance, the self-driving cars were not yet in circulation, nor could the exact time and location of major earthquakes be predicted 15 minutes prior to their occurrence.

Let me first introduce myself. My name is James Eaton. I was thirty-five years old then, a mystery writer, married without kids. And yes, it all started with the cursed bet.

My friend Jacob Barrstein and I were hanging out at our favorite L.A. sports bar one evening at the beginning of February, over eight years ago, where he kept texting back and forth with his girlfriend, Holly, while obviously researching something online. It was irritating as hell; his preoccupation interfered with our conversation.

When he finally tucked the phone away, I said, "We can't even function without our gadgets. Life has become one big technological mess."

He shrugged and replied, "Oh, it's doable. Our parents lived their first 30 years without computers, smartphones, tablets, GPS's, and the like."

"I disagree. I bet you a thousand bucks you can't find a dozen people who are willing to give them up for just a week!" I insisted.

"You're on!"

We talked about other stuff that evening; our main subject being the NHL hockey teams, and how well the Los Angeles Kings and Anaheim Ducks had played lately. Jacob had gone to UCLA and rooted for the Bruins, whereas my college days had been spent at USC, which naturally made me a Trojans fan. We hassled one another during football season, all in good fun. As for baseball and basketball, we both cheered on the Dodgers and Lakers, and kept an open mind about soccer.

Before we went home that evening he said, "How about getting a group together and spending a week away from civilization? No gadgets allowed."

"That's being done all the time on reality TV," I replied.

"Oh, those shows are staged. I'm sure they have medical teams on stand-by, and how 'rugged' can the situation get with camera crews following people around? No, our adventure will be just man versus nature!"

"You're serious about this?"

He grinned and said, "I want to win the thousand dollar bet! Besides, it'll be fun."

I was skeptical and pointed out, "Even if you find a dozen people willing to give it a try, how are you going to enforce the no-gadget thing? I mean, they may have good intentions, but when put to the test, lack the needed discipline."

"Don't worry! I'll lay down the rules beforehand, making sure everyone understands them when committing to our venture."

"When you said 'a week away from civilization,' what exactly did you have in mind?"

"A camping trip, of course. The old-fashioned way in the wild, without any campers or motorhomes; just simple tents."

I stayed silent, watching the hockey game in progress on the big-screen TV. I tried to come up with more objections to Jacob's idea but could not think of any.

After a couple of minutes he said, "So? Are you in?"

"I guess," I replied.

He extended his hand and I shook it, sealing the pact.

Within the next few weeks, we planned a camping trip with roughly 12 people, choosing an isolated spot in the rugged Angeles National Forest, away from any public campground. Or rather, Jacob planned it and I gave my consent, and between the two of us we would finance the entire excursion. He posted the idea on Facebook, mentioning that the first ten "friends" who responded would get a free mountain camping trip. He explained that the point was to have a "roughing it" experience in the wild without any help from electronic gadgets. He stated on his Facebook post, "Don't bother to apply if you are not willing to camp in the true pioneer spirit. Sneaking in any kind of 21st century electronic devices, such as computers, smartphones, tablets, Nintendo DS's, electronic games and anything else along that line, will get you kicked out."

Working as manager at Jock Master Sporting Goods, my pal was able to rent tents and other equipment at a ridiculously low price. We picked the first week in April to execute our bet, which gave us two months to get organized and provide our "guests" with ample time to prepare for the trip.

CHAPTER 2

I was awake long before the alarm clock went off on Monday, April 1, the day of our departure. The date marked the 10th anniversary of my mother's passing and - - as with every 1st of April in the last decade - - evoked guilt, regret, and most of all anger in me. If I hadn't taken a wrong turn and lost my sense of direction that night on the drive to UCLA Medical Center, I'd have arrived at her deathbed in time and been given a chance to reconcile. As it stood, she died with a lot of hostility between us.

I glanced over at Tala, still sound asleep, with appreciation. She was the best thing that had ever happened to me. Beautiful, caring, down-to-earth, and wise beyond words. My only unfulfilled wish was to start a family. We had not been ready to have kids for a long time after we were married, and only began considering the idea a couple of years ago. And now it wasn't happening. There was still plenty of time before Tala's biological clock would give out, so I tried not to be concerned.

The alarm sounded and Tala stirred, murmuring "You didn't sleep well?"

"It's the 1st of April."

"I see."

"I know you think I'm being ridiculous."

Wide awake now, she switched on the nightstand lamp, sat straight up in bed, and looking me in the eye, stated, "Let it go! You've tortured yourself long enough. So your mother died before you could make peace. It's a fact of life and fretting over it is not going to change anything. And who would have expected her to die of complications from pneumonia in the first place? I never understood why you were only notified after her condition worsened and she was placed in ICU."

Not missing a beat, she continued, "Another thing you don't seem to be aware of, what makes you so sure that she would have acknowledged your attempt at reconciliation?"

"Oh, I'm positive she'd have accepted my apology."

"Apology for what, James? Could you possibly apologize for having a different view from hers on just about everything, starting with personal ethics all the way to politics?"

She did not wait for an answer and went on, "And what about the main issue? Her biggest gripe was with me. She didn't approve of me, having set higher aspirations for her son than marrying a mere Filipina nurse. She despised me from day one. After all, I was to blame for your breaking off the engagement with the woman she favored. The fact that I'm Catholic didn't help either. Face it, James, she was a rich bitch, believing that she could change your mind by cutting you out of her will."

I did not comment, knowing deep down that she was right.

Tala suddenly leaned toward me, and offering a kiss, said, "I'm sorry about your mom, but this guilt obsession of yours seems to get worse as time passes. You have no cause to feel guilty. Get it out of your system."

She kissed me again and said, "Cheer up, already."

I gave her a halfhearted grin.

Then, straightening and getting out of bed she stated, "Now, let's get ready for that big camping adventure of yours!" She added, "Wear my favorite blue polo shirt, the one that brings out the deep blue of your eyes."

I perked up and said, "I'm so glad you're able to take the week off and decided to come."

"Well, I'm counting on a relaxing time to focus on our efforts in the baby-making department!"

CHAPTER 3

We met in the Jock Master Sporting Goods parking lot in the San Fernando Valley on that mild and sunny spring morning. Jacob had an agreement with the store owners to leaving the group's individual cars parked on their lot for the week. The idea was that we would all drive up in Jacob's van and my SUV. He had hooked up an enclosed small cargo trailer to his van, loaded with food and water, as well as tents and other camping gear. Air mattresses and sleeping bags were stored on his roof luggage carrier.

We got there early and found Jacob already waiting for us. He greeted Tala with, "Great to have you along. I couldn't persuade Holly to join us; she's a high maintenance sort of woman." He chuckled, "Her words: 'I'll take sleeping in a comfortable bed, hot showers, and microwaving my food any day over your nature hunt!'"

The rest of our campers arrived in pairs or alone, and Jacob checked them off his attendance

list. I had not met any of these people before and I
don't think that even Jacob knew our guests well.
There was a blue-collar guy in his early thirties by
the name of Todd; Marcelo, a kid of twenty-one;
The Kim family - Yon and Min with their six-year-
old little boy Mikey; a lesbian couple Hannah and
London; and brothers Derek and Curtis, a pair of
rednecks in their mid-twenties.

Jacob was pissed when the Kims showed up
with a young child. He whispered to me, "I had
no idea. I hope they don't expect us to play little
kids games."

We had loaded everyone's backpack and the
booster car seat for Mikey into our respective
vehicles, and people were ready to step into the
cars when Jacob said, "Candie Valentina and her
friend Nicklaus aren't here yet."

I said, "You're kidding. *The* Candie Valentina.
As in Hollywood?"

"Yep, her."

As the group was getting antsy, Jacob said,
"Dammit. Marcelo took the train and a bus,
and managed to get here on time, so why can't
Candie and her friend?" Checking his watch, he
continued, "I give them five more minutes and if
they don't show, we'll leave without them."

We already had our motors running when a
late-model Mercedes-Benz tore into the parking
lot at high speed. Candie leaned out the driver's
side window, hollering, "Looks like I've made it
just in time. I'll follow you!"

Jacob turned off the engine, got out of the car and said, "As agreed, we're only taking the van and the SUV. So park your car and hop in."

She argued, "No offense, but I refuse to leave my car in this lot for a week. Besides, I'm sure there isn't room in your vehicles for my two suitcases and a carry-on."

Jacob asked, "Where is Nicklaus?"

Hearing his name, a black poodle stuck his head out the back window and let out a happy bark.

"You're taking a dog along? You must be out of your mind!"

Jacob stepped closer to Candie's Mercedes and they argued some more, but I could not hear what was said. Judging by the way he gesticulated with his hand, there appeared to be a fierce battle of wills. Then he seemed to give in and walked back to his van shouting, "I bet you have a built-in GPS in the car."

She promised, "I'll keep it turned off."

And so we caravanned to our destination, with Jacob leading the way in the van, followed by my SUV, and Candie's Mercedes bringing up the rear. I could already tell that Candie Valentina was going to be a pain in the ass.

CHAPTER 4

Except for Jacob and me, nobody knew the exact location of our camping spot in the mountains. I doubt that I could have easily found it on my own, even though Jacob had driven me up once. He, on the other hand, had gone there many times, carefully picking just the right site for our purpose. He had done the law-abiding thing by obtaining a National Forest Adventure Pass, which gave us permission to park our vehicles along the road and set up camp. Being the conscientious planner, he had also applied for, and was in possession of, a Campfire Permit.

Todd, the brothers Derek and Curtis, as well as Hannah and London were riding with Jacob, and we had the Kim family and Marcelo in our car. Yon and Min Kim did not say much on the ride, even though Tala tried several times to engage them in conversation. They answered her questions politely but did not volunteer any extra comments. There might have been a language barrier, I thought, or maybe they were just shy and needed to warm up to us. Later, as we got to know them better, it became clear that their English was indeed fine and they weren't bashful. Min and especially Yon just happened to be quiet folks by nature. Their little boy Mikey was clearly excited about the camping trip and asked, "Are we there yet?" every ten minutes.

As we left the foothills behind and started the ascent into the forest on Big Tujunga Canyon Road, I took up the role of tour guide, saying, "We could have gone up Highway 2, also known as Angeles Crest Highway, but this access road is closer coming from the Valley."

Then I pointed out, "After the Station Fire that raged in these San Gabriel Mountains for two weeks, starting at the end of August in 2009, this road was closed until December of that year when it re-opened to through traffic. But it wasn't until the end of May, 2012 - nearly three years after the fire - that it finally re-opened for business, meaning for the general public to enjoy the area for recreation. The Station Fire burned over 160,000 acres and was the largest wildfire of Los Angeles County in modern history, killing two firefighters."

We soon found out that Marcelo was a talker. He kept us entertained for a good part of the way. We learned that he was from Chile, attending college here in Southern California, that he didn't own a car and got around on his bicycle, that he shared an apartment with two other students, and that he enjoyed our food, cheeseburgers being his favorite, and loved American TV, but not the commercials. His English was formal and excellent.

The curvy mountain passage led through rocky areas on either side of the road, and after turning left onto the Angeles Forest Highway, the road became even steeper and the scenery more rugged. And all along the way there was evidence of burned trees and brush. Whether this was still damage from the Station Fire or a more recent wildfire was beyond the extent of my knowledge.

When we had traveled approximately 30 miles into the Angeles Forest, we passed the small access road leading down to the Monte Cristo Campground. We glimpsed a couple of tents and a motorhome while passing by. I looked at the child passenger in the rear view mirror and said, "We're almost there now!"

About three miles farther, we had arrived at our destination. The ride up from Foothill Boulevard in Sunland had taken less than an hour, and yet the landscape looked isolated and far from civilization.

There was a turnout in the road and beyond it a good-sized flat area, perfect for erecting tents. Parking the van and SUV parallel to each other was no problem, and there was barely enough space, but Candie managed to squeeze her car in behind mine. We got out, stretched, and then explored the piece of land that was to become our home for the next week. We could hear but not see a stream. Tala and I walked the length of the plateau and looked down the canyon. Sure enough, there was a creek about 30 yards below us.

Tala looked at the mountain ranges all around us and exclaimed, "This place is gorgeous! And not a cloud in the sky."

We ate our lunches of pre-made peanut-butter-and-jelly sandwiches, sitting on the ground, and then went about setting up camp. Jacob allotted the four two-person tents to the Kim family, Hannah and London, Candie and her dog, and Tala and me. He shared his big tent with Todd, Marcelo, Derek and Curtis.

Jacob unhooked the cargo trailer and with the combined efforts of his "tent buddies" managed to pull and push it to the center of the clearing, where they put up the six-person dome tent. The rest of us pitched our two-person A-frame tents in a semi-circle around theirs.

So far, the dog Nicklaus - - or Nick, as I preferred calling him - - was no problem at all. While the adults kept busy getting settled, little Mikey entertained Nick by playing the game of "throw and fetch" with the poodle's tennis ball. Neither the dog nor the boy seemed to tire of the repetitive activity.

Tala and I found a flat surface, cleared away sticks, stones, and other debris, and then went to work. First we laid our tent out on the ground where we planned on setting it up. Assembling the poles by connecting the pole segments was easy. To put up the tent, we placed a pole at each end of the tent, lifting the pole straight up while putting the bottom of the pole into the ground. Then we fastened it to the ground by hammering stakes into the loops at each corner and side, making sure that the fabric was stretched tight. Next, we pulled the guy-ropes out and secured them to the ground, using a peg. The guy-ropes needed to be pulled taut to keep the tent from falling over in case of strong wind. Finally, we placed the flysheet over the top, aligning the corners with the tent's ends, and then secured the flysheet guy-ropes tightly to the ground with pegs.

We stepped back to admire our handiwork and nodded in satisfaction. I looked around to see how everyone else was doing. The Kims to our right were almost done with their set-up, and it looked like Hannah and London, who occupied the spot next to them, had finished theirs. The guys assigned to the dome tent were still busy setting up, except for Todd, who seemed to be single-handedly pitching Candie's tent to our left, while she watched.

I thought, so the prima donna among us has already found a willing victim!

Later, I was coming back from getting our backpacks out of the car when all hell broke loose. Apparently, Jacob had caught Candie about to text on her smartphone and he totally lost his cool, going into a rage.

He shouted, "What the hell are you doing? How arrogant and undermining! Not only did you drive up in your own car and bring luggage for an army when my instructions were one backpack per person, but you are in violation of our main goal of this venture: no gadgets!"

She murmured, "I just wanted to let my agent know where I'm at."

"Oh, I get it. You were planning to have the paparazzi catch you up here for a publicity stunt. Over my dead body!" And he grabbed the smartphone out of her hand, ran the entire distance of the clearing, all the way to the edge of the cliff, and flung it down the mountain.

I let him cool down before I walked over and smirked, "Theoretically, you've already lost the bet."

He stared at me.

"Candie didn't *willingly* give up her gadget."

"Let's not split hairs over this. Willingly or not, she was *about* to use the phone but actually never did. Besides, I'm not even sure whether there's reception up here."

"Fair enough," I said. "The bet's still on."

CHAPTER 5

By mid-afternoon, everyone was pretty much settled and Jacob called us all to gather in front of his tent.

He asked, "Are there any other devices I should know about?"

Hannah said "I brought a camera. Is that allowed?"

"What kind of camera?"

"Just an old-fashioned one, not part of a phone."

"You may use it. Anyone else?"

Nobody spoke up.

"Good! I'll walk you briefly through the rules before letting you explore the area on your own. First off, let me remind you that we are a team and share the responsibility of chores. James and I are providing food and drinks, but we all take turns with the cooking and washing of dishes. There is obviously no running water, so we haul it up from the nearby stream for doing the dishes.

"Here is how it's done: We fill a large can with water and carry it to the campsite. Then we pour it into two plastic wash bins, one for soapy water, the other for rinsing. When finished, the water is dumped into bushes, but far away from the creek in order not to contaminate it. We also brush our teeth up here; you can either use bottled water sparingly or fill a cup with creek water and carry it up."

He went on, "Our personal bathing may be done in the stream, but without soap, shampoo or the like. In other words, a quick dip or rinse."

Candie burst out, "You've got to be kidding! The water must be freezing."

Jacob grinned and replied, "Yes it's cold, but good for the complexion."

Hannah said, "Wouldn't it be easier to use paper plates and cups rather than going through the trouble of doing dishes?"

"No, that's not an option. We need to make as little trash as possible. Everything we brought up will go home with us again, including our trash. We are not leaving a single scrap of paper or other waste behind."

Pointing to the north end of our campsite, he went on, "Speaking of waste, I placed a port-a-potty behind those bushes over there. You'll find instructions attached; please read them carefully."

Curtis said, "And we take turns emptying the toilet too?"

"You got it," Jacob replied. Then he continued his orientation monologue, "As far as safety goes, don't go hiking alone; there should always be at least one person along. Wild animals tend not to attack humans in groups. I am going to give you each a US Forest Service safety whistle. Take it along when leaving our camp, even when going down to the stream to bathe. Do not misuse it and only blow into it when you need help, as the whistle is extremely loud. I'll also give you each a small first aid kit. Always take sun protection and windbreakers along on hikes. There is no prediction of rain in the weather forecast for this week, but temperatures can vary from one hour to the next. I also must stress that it's important to get back to our camp area before nightfall. It's too dangerous to trek around in the dark. "

London asked, "What kind of wild animals?"

"There are coyotes, mountain lions, and even bears in the Angeles National Forest, but they generally only attack humans when they feel threatened. And now is the time that rattlesnakes come out of hibernation. I have a snake-bite kit in my tent."

He glared at Candie and ordered, "Keep your dog leashed at all times on a hike. We can't afford him chasing after wildlife."

"More likely that the wildlife would be chasing Nick," I remarked, and got a good laugh out of the group, except for Candie, who shot an annoyed glance my way.

Jacob continued, "As far as scavenging bears are concerned, we keep our food stored in the van with the windows up at night. Did any of you bring extra food along?"

Min said, "I brought cookies."

"Anyone else?"

When no others spoke up, Jacob urged Min to give him the cookies in the evening and he would store them overnight. He gave more instructions, but over eight years later, I cannot recall them all.

As we disbursed, I overheard one of the brothers saying to the other, "He sure takes himself seriously!"

His bro laughed and shot back, "Must be hard for you not to be in command!"

While the rest of our group went to explore the grounds around our campsite, Jacob, Todd, and I built a campfire pit. We chose a location a good distance away from the tents or any trees. Since we only had one shovel, Jacob and Todd took turns digging the pit, and I gathered enough medium-sized rocks to form a circle about three feet in diameter. When they had dug approximately 12 inches deep, we placed the rocks around the perimeter of our fire pit. Then we filled the pit two-thirds full with dry kindling and firewood, which Jacob had brought from home in case dead wood was scarce. We kept the shovel and a bucket I had filled with water from the creek handy so that we could quickly extinguish the fire should it threaten to get out of control.

Now all was ready for the evening's entertainment.

CHAPTER 6

Thanks to Jock Master Sporting Goods, we had a camp stove and also a camp grill at our disposal. Jacob and Marcelo took up kitchen duty for our first dinner. We watched as Jacob put a prime rib roast on the grill while Marcelo boiled a big pot of water on the burner for corn on the cob and buttered the garlic bread. The mood of the group was upbeat in anticipation of a delicious meal and a fun-filled week of camp life.

Meanwhile, I started the campfire, and when the food was ready, we sat in folding camp chairs in a circle around the fire and savored every bite.

Jacob chuckled and said, "Don't expect such a feast every night. This is a launch party, but from here on out, we'll live on pasta, rice, and potatoes. Meat or fish - -if any - - will come in a can."

He opened a couple of bottles of Merlot, adding, "And the wine is a one-time-only treat too. Starting tomorrow, we'll drink water."

Min, Hannah, and of course little Mikey passed on the Merlot, so that there was just enough for one glass each. That we drank out of plastic goblets didn't spoil taste buds nor ambience. For dessert we roasted marshmallows. The aroma of burning wood and the crackling sound of the fire put us all in a relaxed state.

Jacob said, "Now is the time to get acquainted. Except for my friend James and his wife Tala, I don't know any of you well and none of you know one another. So let's do introductions - - first names only - - and tell a little something about ourselves."

He cleared his throat and said, "I'll go first. My name is Jacob. I manage a sporting goods store, am not married but have a serious girlfriend at home, and I arranged this camping trip because James and I have a bet going. He claims that a group of a dozen modern people cannot last a week without any electronic gadgets, and I'm about to prove him wrong."

I was next and stated, "I'm James, married to my Tala here," nudging her playfully. "I'm a mystery writer by profession. I think we should all mention how we know Jacob. He and I met years ago when serving on a jury that seemed to last forever. We clicked right away and stayed buddies after the trial was over. Tala and I often double date with Jacob and his girlfriend, Holly. You heard from Jacob why I'm here."

My wife said, "I'm Tala, a nurse, and I came along to make sure James doesn't get bored," and she smiled at me.

"You have an unusual name. I like the sound of it," London remarked.

"It is Filipino and means bright star."

Next to her sat the brothers Derek, with his head shaved, and Curtis, sporting a full head of curly hair pulled into a ponytail. Derek spoke for both of them, saying, "Me and Curtis work in our old man's pawn shop. We are both single and available. We bicker a lot on the job and part of the reason we came on this trip is to try to get along and become closer. I know Jacob from the Sierra Mountaineering Club."

Now it was the Kim family's turn to introduce themselves. Yon stated, "We are pleased to be here. I am Yon, originally from South Korea. I own a convenience store in Alhambra. I met Jacob at a CSBA convention."

Candie asked, "What's that?"

"California Small Business Association," he replied.

The boy who sat between his parents said, "I'm Mikey and a first grader. I'm here because Mommy made me come."

Everyone burst out laughing.

His mom spoke up, "I'm Min, a stay-at-home mom, active in the PTA. I teach piano and violin out of our home. And it is true, we are here because Mikey is already addicted to video games, and we thought a week away from them and fresh air will do him good."

The college student was next and he said, "My name is Marcelo and I come from Chile. I am a junior at the University of Southern California, where I am majoring in physics. I joined this group because I would like to get the American experience outside of campus life. I am on spring break, so the timing is right for me. I met Jacob at his store when he sold me my mountain bike."

He looked over at Jacob, the expression in his dark eyes amused, as he added, "Since Yon mentioned the CSBA convention, I realize that you are an entrepreneur. At the time I thought you were an employee of the sporting goods store."

Jacob replied, "I'm just the manager, not owner. My boss was unable to attend the convention and sent me in his place."

"I see." Marcelo faced the group again and continued, "Jacob and I had a long conversation at the store and it turned out that he had visited Chile and even stayed in the town I'm from. It's a small world, isn't it? So we kept in touch via Facebook."

Candie commented, "Sounds like you're a smart cookie and your parents must be rich to afford sending you to school in the States, to USC no less."

He seemed flustered by her rude remark, or maybe he was just in awe of her, but he answered politely in his meticulous English, "I obtained a scholarship and availed myself of the International Financial Aid package."

Candie patted his arm and remarked, "Good job, Sweetie!" Then she said, "Guess it's my turn and I'm sure you all know who I am."

I could not believe her arrogance and looked over at the Kim family. Their faces, illuminated by the campfire, showed that they had no clue as to who she was. So I said, "Tell us, just in case."

She shrugged, gave her blonde mane a flip and announced, "I'm Candie Valentina, a stage and film actress. I'm divorced, in no relationship at the moment, and Nicklaus here is my best friend."

The poodle, who had been sitting quietly next to his owner staring into the flames, stood up as she mentioned his name and happily wagged his tail. She petted him, settling him down again, and then went on, "I am in between jobs right now, and yes, I admit it, my initial idea was to maybe get a bit of publicity out of this."

She looked over at Jacob and asked, "Am I forgiven?"

"Yes, if you have no more stunts up your sleeve, that is."

"Cross my heart!" Then she addressed the rest of us again and continued, "Even though I hadn't seen Jacob in years, we go back a long way. We actually went to high school together."

Jacob grinned and said, "That was before you changed your name. In those days you were Candie Leutenegger."

She shot him an angry glance, clearly not pleased by his disclosure, but recovered fast and said, "Wouldn't anyone change it with a name like that?"

Todd, who sat on Candie's other side and had openly admired her all day, came to her rescue by quickly changing the subject, asking, "Why did you name your dog Nicklaus?"

"I got him last Christmas."

He scratched Nick under the chin and said, "So you're still a puppy." Then he turned his attention back to the rest of us, giving his profile. "I'm Todd, single, a roofer, and happy to get a free vacation. My connection with Jacob is also through the Sierra Mountaineering Club."

Out of all the guys in the group, Todd and Jacob were the most muscular. But whereas Jacob achieved it by working out, Todd's muscle tone came naturally by doing manual work.

That left the lesbian couple. They were both of average height and slender. Hannah, a wavy-haired brunette, had an outgoing personality. She gave her name and then said, "I am a physical therapist and plan to marry London in June. We love the outdoors, and when I learned about this trip from Jacob's Facebook post, we thought it might be lots of fun. I was seeing Jacob professionally, treating him with physical therapy when he threw his back out, and afterwards we stayed in touch."

London, ash blonde and wearing glasses, was a tad reserved. She simply said, "I'm a ghostwriter and look forward to hiking in these mountains. My association with Jacob is through Hannah."

Curtis gave her an appreciative stare and said, "How about if I take you up on your services. I have a great idea for a futuristic science fiction book."

"Derek cut in and said, "Never mind him. His ideas are mostly a manic jumble. You can't take him seriously."

His brother shot back, " And you are such a bore with no ideas at all." Then he winked at London and said, "We could have a great writing future together!"

Hannah said, "Watch your step, Curtis."

"Just kidding!"

CHAPTER 7

I threw another log on the fire and was close enough to overhear Marcelo and Todd's conversation with Candie. They praised her starring performances in a number of films. The guys were obviously big fans and she gobbled it all up. There was no denying she was a looker with a body to match, but in my opinion, her acting was limited to flirty airhead roles. And since I had just learned that she was 32 - - having gone to high school with Jacob - - soon she would be too old for those parts. While she flirted with the two men, Nick plopped himself next to Mikey, who had his own private talk with the dog.

As for me, London remarked that she had read a couple of my books and praised my ability of combining an intelligent plot with interesting characters. She was especially impressed with *Stifle Her Scream* and congratulated me on its making the bestseller list in January. I have to admit that I was pleased. I asked her about her ghostwriting and learned that she wrote memoirs for famous people, or just common folks with an interesting story to tell. She gave a few examples of personalities she had met and places visited in the course of her work. She also shared that she was in the process of writing her own novel.

And so we talked shop for a while. London wanted to know if I outlined my mysteries, and I answered that I did not. I explained that when starting to write a new manuscript, I had a general idea of the plot, knew who the villain was, had a motive for the murder, and was familiar with the chosen location. The rest would all fall into place as I wrote the story and immersed myself into the minds of the characters. Naturally, after that first draft, I would write a second, and a third, going over chapter after chapter, revising and editing.

She asked, "Don't you even take notes?"

"Yes, I will take notes on occasion. I do a lot of plotting in my head while driving, going for walks, during meals, in short, all the time. I've been known to exit the freeway, pull over to the side of the road, and write things down when having a sudden clever idea."

"What did you mean by saying you were familiar with the location?"

"I do all my research in person, traveling to the destinations I choose for my stories."

She nodded, and asked no more.

I was suddenly aware that all kept quiet for a while, gazing into the flames of the campfire, enjoying the peace and serenity of the moment.

Then, Candie, ever the troublemaker, turned to Derek and Curtis and asked loud enough for all to hear, "So what do you boys bicker about?"

Curtis said, "Derek bosses me around and is a know-it-all."

"And you never listen," his brother shot back. "You're incompetent and let customers run you. You have no idea what stuff is worth, so we often take a loss because of you. The worst part is that you never learn from your mistakes. When I point something out to you, instead of being grateful for the advice, you start a fight. But we both know the real reason you're always looking for a fight; you can't stand it that I'm our old man's favorite."

Curtis snarled, "That's a bunch of crap!"

He was about to pounce on his older brother when Jacob intervened and loudly suggested we tell spooky ghost stories. No one took him up on it, but it calmed the brothers down.

Then he had another idea and said, "What's funny about today's date?"

We failed to get his meaning.

Todd finally burst out, "Of course, it's April Fools day! I'm surprised none of you thought of fooling anyone!"

The observation prompted Jacob to propose that we all take turns sharing anecdotes of April

Fools pranks we made in the past. Again, no one seemed eager to volunteer a prank tale, so Jacob started with his.

CHAPTER 8

Jacob began, "This happened a long time ago when I was a senior in college. I had a practical joker friend who teased me on a regular basis for never having the guts to play pranks on people. On an April Fools day, there was road construction going on near the campus, with traffic being directed to detours. After the construction workers had left for the day, my pal and I happened to walk by one of the detour signs. On a whim I said, 'What if I turned the arrow sign around for an April Fools joke?' He dared me to do it and I went ahead while he stood guard, making sure no one was watching. The task was not without effort - - I had to unscrew the sign from the post it was attached to, turn it around and screw it back on - - but I managed it before anyone was the wiser. Originally, the arrow for the detour pointed left, and after I had turned the sign upside down, it pointed to the right.

Obviously, we didn't stick around to watch, but could picture the traffic confusion this caused."

He grinned and ended his story with, "The next day, there was an article in the local paper blaming the road workers for the mix-up. So I was home free with the prank."

He looked around our circle and said, "I'm sure many of you have an April Fools story to tell."

Hannah said, "I just remembered one. It was in high school. We had this math teacher who always started his class with, 'Who did not do the homework?' And then he gave hell to the students who hadn't done it. Well, on that occasion, we all raised our hands. He got bright red in the face with rage, stamped his foot, and yelled, 'The entire class didn't do their homework? What is going on? I'll hand out detention to each and every one of you!' In unison, all of us students got to our feet and shouted, 'April Fool!'"

Marcelo spoke up, "I did a prank, like you call it, but it was not in April and it did not go as planned."

"Doesn't matter; we're ready to hear any good story," Jacob assured him.

Marcelo became animated, telling his story in a comical way. He recounted, "We were altar boys, Orlando and I, and usually scheduled to serve together. Orlando had this habit of nipping into the altar wine. Just a few sips, so nobody was the wiser. One day, I decided to teach him a lesson and added vinegar to an almost empty bottle. I already pictured him taking a good swig and imagined his expression when swallowing the sour mixture.

"To my horror, his parents called him in sick that Sunday and the adult verger took his place. There was no way I could get rid of the wine laced with vinegar. When the priest drank it during mass, he had a coughing fit and almost choked to death. Of course, I was found out and punished."

Candie exclaimed, "Oh, I have a good one! This dates back to the time before I was well known, when I had to hustle every step of the way. I auditioned for this part I wanted so badly it hurt. Being only about the tenth person they had interviewed so far, I was confident of getting the part, until I saw the long line of women on my way out. The queue stretched along half the outside of the building. I suddenly had a brainstorm. Pretending to be a person in charge, I announced, 'Attention, everyone! The auditions are over for today. Try again tomorrow. I repeat: Today's auditions are cancelled.' I feigned going back into the building. Then, as the women went away, I made myself get lost in the crowd."

Min said, "That really wasn't nice."

"Well, it's a cutthroat business."

Todd asked, "Did you get the part?"

"Actually, no. But I was a close runner up."

Everyone kept silent for a while. The only sound came from the occasional crackle of the fire as we stared into it.

Todd suddenly laughed and said, "Here is my contribution of antics. This wasn't all that long ago, two years tops. I spent a weekend with my buddies on the Colorado River. Needless to say that we all had a beer or two. One of the guys went skinny dipping."

Mikey asked, "What's skinny dipping?" His mom whispered something to him which made the little boy giggle.

Todd continued, "When the guy came out of the river, his clothes weren't where he'd left them. Just for fun, we'd hung them from a tree some distance away. As he started walking toward the tree, cussing us out nonstop, a couple of chicks on horseback came wading along the river's edge. There was nothing but open land between him and his pants, so he had no choice but to head back into the water."

Todd laughed out loud when he added, "I'll never forget the hilarious sight of him turning around in panic and running back into the river, holding on to his junk!"

Tala told her prank tale of having sewed up her home-economics teacher's jacket sleeve so that the lady's arm got stuck when she tried to don the garment. This was no news to me; I had heard the story before.

Jacob tried to get more mischievous stories from the group but the subject had run dry. The serious Yon stated, "I don't do pranks; that's for children." His wife nodded in agreement. London said, "Count me out too," and Derek commented, "We see a lot of weirdoes coming into our shop, trying to sell or pawn all kinds of bizarre stuff, but I can't think of a prank off hand."

Curtis said, "Oh, I remember something I did for a joke once. It wasn't exactly playing a prank on any one person, but it was hilarious. I taped magnets to the bottom of my coffee cup, put it on the roof of my car, and drove around town. When other drivers or pedestrians pointed frantically at the top of my car, I smiled and did the Queen Elizabeth wave."

His brother rolled his eyes and remarked, "That is just the kind of dumbass thing you'd find funny."

Before the brothers got a chance to be at each other's throats again, Jacob intervened. Looking straight at me, trying to butter me up, he coaxed, "Come on James. Let's hear it from you, the ultimate story teller!"

I wasn't in the mood and shook my head.

"Come on, be a good sport," he insisted, and I gave in.

I said, "I agree with Yon, playing practical jokes is for kids. My tale is not about me being the prankster, but about others playing a prank on me. It happened at Boy Scout camp when I was 12 years old. One night, I woke up in panic out of a deep sleep, but it was too late. I had already peed in the bed. To my horror, several of my fellow scouts stood by my cot, laughing their heads off.

Later, one of the boys admitted that they'd waited until I was sound asleep, then dipped my fingers into a bowl of warm water, making my muscles relax so that I had let go. To this day, I fight going to sleep when hearing running water, or even when just thinking of water."

Someone said, "Good luck with the stream up here!"

The campfire gathering soon broke up, and we made sure that the fire was completely extinguished before turning in. It was too dark and too late to wash dishes; Jacob and Marcelo left them to do first thing in the morning.

CHAPTER 9

Snug inside our sleeping bags that first night, Tala remarked, "That was the best prime rib I've ever tasted!" And after a pause, "Let's volunteer to cook the spaghetti dinner tomorrow."

"Sure."

Then she said, "What an eclectic group of people we are!"

"That's not surprising, considering we live in Southern California and are used to mingling with folks from all walks of life."

She snickered and said, "We may be an interesting bunch, but I doubt that Marcelo will get his 'American experience' out of us! And Curtis sure has a short fuse. I wouldn't want to get on his bad side."

"Both brothers are temperamental and seem to have a sibling rivalry," I said.

"Hush, listen," Tala whispered.

A female voice with perfect pitch rang out from the tent next to ours. The sound was sweet and clear as a bell. We listened spellbound to the unusual melody and the foreign words.

When the singing stopped, Tala said, "How lovely! That must have been Min, singing a Korean lullaby to Mikey. The Kims sure are a dignified couple and their little boy is sweet. Did you see how the dog immediately took to him?"

"I did."

She was quiet for a couple of minutes and then said, "Some of the prank stories were entertaining. I especially enjoyed listening to Marcelo. He is a good story teller. I didn't care for Candie's, though. Too spiteful for my taste."

There is no cattiness in Tala, so I was surprised when she continued, "That woman is full of herself and thinks she can get her way by batting her eyes and tossing her blonde mane simply because she is Candie Valentina."

"Seems to work for Todd and Marcelo," I said.

"I can understand it in Todd's case, but what could a brain like Marcelo and her possibly talk about?"

I said, "Get real! He may be majoring in physics, but I doubt he'd be interested in discussing the quantum theory."

"The attraction must be strictly physical."

"Good guess, Tala, considering that he is a 21-year-old male with hormones at their peak."

She ignored my sarcasm and continued, "And did you see what Candie was wearing?"

As a writer I try to notice detail, but, like most men, fail to pay attention to clothing. I admitted, "No."

"Well, let's just say that her outfit was by no means appropriate for camping."

I changed the subject and remarked, "I had an interesting talk with London. I never gave much thought to ghostwriting, but she made me aware that the job can be interesting and fulfilling."

Tala remarked, "Hannah sure is protective of her. Did you see how she pounced on Curtis when he made that silly comment to London?"

"I would react the same way if he'd try to hit on you."

"I can take care of myself, thank you! And what he said can hardly be called 'hitting on her.' He just tried to be funny."

"He'd better watch his mouth in the future, though."

There was a long stillness again, then she suddenly said, "You never told me that you were a Boy Scout nor the rest of that episode."

"Oh, I wasn't a Boy Scout and the peeing in my bed thing never happened. I made it all up since I'm better at telling fiction than true stories."

Tala giggled and said, "You were the real prankster tonight, fooling everyone!"

Then she said, "It's been a long day. I'm bushed," kissed me good night, zipped her sleeping bag up to her neck, and was gone in a matter of seconds.

I wished that sleep could have come that easy to me. It may have been the heavy meal, or the way fragments of the day's events popped into my mind, it certainly was not the distant sound of the creek - - after all, I had made the running water thing up - - but I spent another sleep-deprived night for the second time in a row.

CHAPTER 10

At the crack of dawn I heard faint sounds coming from the big tent and realized it was useless trying for more shut-eye. Judging by her regular breathing, I knew that Tala was still in dreamland. As noiseless as possible, I eased out of the sleeping bag, found the pants I'd worn the day before, grabbed my toiletry bag, and quietly left the tent.

Trekking down the steep hillside to the creek, I was treated to a gorgeous sunrise with the promise of another perfect spring day. I passed Marcelo, who was on his way back from the stream. The young man happily whistled a tune while carrying up water for cleaning dishes. I found Jacob by the creek, washing up. We had a word or two, and then I went farther down the stream to take a sponge bath. Bathing in the small creek, to use Jacob's word, required a stretch of the imagination. The water was ice cold, making me catch my breath.

Hiking back up, I came across the pawn shop brothers and spotted Candie a distance away, taking Nick on an early morning walk. By the tents, the rest of the campers seemed to have come to life, ready for a new day of adventure.

The continental breakfast was a do-it-yourself deal with bread, butter, jelly and cheese at the ready. A big pot with simmering water sat on the stove burner so that people could help themselves to instant coffee or tea bags.

Jacob asked, "Is Candie still asleep?"

"No," I replied. "I saw her earlier; she must not be back from walking Nick."

After breakfast he said, "Is everyone in the mood for hiking up to Mill Creek Summit and then taking the Pacific Crest trail to Pacifico Mountain? We can pack a picnic lunch."

We all answered in the affirmative, even though none of us had the slightest idea as to the location of these places or how long of a hike was involved.

"Okay," he said, "I'll fetch the food," and went to get it from the van.

Seconds later, he came rushing back empty handed and I could already tell from a distance that he was fuming.

He hollered, "She's gone!"

We all stared at him, baffled.

"Candie took off. Her car is gone!"

Everyone was speechless at first. Then people voiced their opinions. "How could she just leave without a word?" "That's really selfish." "She acted natural when turning in last night." "How rude!" "She sure didn't last long." Each person had a different take on Candie's action, but most agreed that it was uncalled for.

Marcelo said, "She must have had a good reason for leaving; let's not judge her prematurely."

"Yeah, give the woman a break, you guys," Todd agreed.

Hannah said, "I can't believe you two! How can you defend her? You sure are under her spell if you can't see what a calculating egotist she is."

Curtis commented, "Now we know why she drove up with her own wheels. The woman figured she'd take off if camp life didn't suit her."

Jacob had calmed down some and came to me, saying, "Guess I've lost the bet."

I said, "I almost feel sorry for you."

After a pause he went on, "There's no reason we can't stay the entire week, though."

"Of course not."

Later, as Jacob handed us each our picnic lunch of beef jerky, trail mix, power bar, and bottled water, a happily panting Nick came running toward us with Candie in tow.

"Where the hell did you go?" Jacob thundered.

Candie smiled sweetly and said, "Oh, did you miss me? I didn't want to wake anybody, figuring I'd be back soon."

"You drove off in your car, so where the frickin' hell did you go?"

"Just down the road to that campground we passed on the way up, to shower."

"Monte Cristo?"

"Yeah, that's the one."

He glared at her and said, "They don't have showers at the Monte Cristo Campground."

"They don't have public ones, but the nice family in the motorhome let me use theirs. Turns out, they are big fans of mine." She beamed and added, "They said that I'm welcome to use the shower every day until Thursday when they're leaving."

Jacob suddenly burst out laughing and said, "Most of us are glad you're back."

And to me, "The bet isn't settled yet!"

CHAPTER 11

It was mid-morning by the time folks had used the port-a-potty, attended to personal hygiene, and packed their backpacks. We started out on the hike as one big group, but soon split into smaller groups according to each person's pace. We trekked upward in a steady climb and when we reached Mill Creek Summit, it became clear that the rest of us could not keep up with Jacob, Derek and Curtis.

I had a hunch that Todd could have also effortlessly stayed in the lead pack but preferred hanging with Candie, a practical decision, since he carried her lunch and water. How Candie hadn't found room in her two suitcases for a backpack was beyond my comprehension. Remembering Tala's comment from the night before, I paid specific attention to what the actress in our midst was wearing. She had on a bright pink fitness outfit. It looked great on her but would have been better suited for wearing inside a gym. To her credit, she'd outfitted herself with brand-new hiking boots. The rest of us were clad in nondescript khaki or gray cargo pants.

Jacob and the brothers waited for the rest of us to catch up by the Mill Creek Summit Forest Service Station, and Marcelo asked, "How far is the hike?"

"From here, about six miles," Jacob replied.

Yon said, "That's 12 miles roundtrip. Adding the mile we walked to this spot and back totals 14 miles. Mikey can't handle that."

"Feel free to go back to our tents now, or turn around any time you like. The hike is optional."

"I should hope so," Curtis snickered.

We ended up in the following marching order: Jacob with the two brothers showing the way, Hannah and London keeping pace a short stretch behind them, followed by Marcelo, Candie with Nick on the leash, and Todd. The Kim family, Tala and I brought up the rear. Before long, we lost sight of the first two groups but got an occasional glimpse of the people immediately ahead of us. Candie's bright outfit especially stood out. Even from a distance I could tell that she had a hard time keeping Nick in line. He was pulling at the leash, obviously wanting to explore and sniff every bush along the way. And who could blame him? The poodle must have felt like he was in dog heaven, having probably never been so close to nature other than a visit to the dog park.

The trail led east at first, giving us an awesome view of Tie Canyon. About three miles into the hike, it turned north through a forest of cone spruce and oak. It was at this point that the Kim family decided to stop for lunch and then turn back to camp.

I asked, "Are you okay with returning on your own?"

"No problem at all," Yon assured me. "After eating our picnic lunch, we can take it slow on the way back."

Tala and I downed a couple of swigs of water before continuing to trek uphill and eventually emerged onto less shaded slopes.

We reached a crest, and on that clear day, the view of the Antelope Valley and Mojave Desert was stunning. I pulled Tala close to me, and we stood in silence, gazing at the panorama stretching out below us.

We were about to round the ridge and turn south when we happened upon Candie, sitting on the ground. Marcelo and Todd, who held on to Nick, stood waiting for her. Getting close, we noticed that Candie had taken one shoe and sock off and was in the process of applying a Band-Aid to her heel.

"A blister?" I asked.

She nodded and said, "Guess I should've worn in my hiking boots at home."

"Want to turn back?"

"Heck no," she replied, "I came this far. Might as well stick it out and go all the way."

So now we were a group of five people again, plus a dog. We headed south where that section of the Pacific Crest Trail intersected a dirt road. The trail followed that road for about half a mile, turned left, and then climbed east again. The last leg we hiked under Jeffrey pines and oaks.

Before we got to the Pacifico Mountain Campground, we met up with Curtis, who came walking back in our direction.

He said, "Can I hang with you guys? I'm tired of Jacob's patronizing."

I asked, "What's your gripe?"

"He won't let me smoke a little pot; said it was a fire hazard. And of course Derek takes his side. I'm sick of 'em both. I'm a responsible adult and resent being treated like a child. Smoking pot is gonna be legalized in California any day now, so what's the big deal?"

I stated, "Sorry, but I have to agree with Jacob. What you do in your own backyard is your business, but up here any type of smoking - - be it regular cigarettes or marijuana - - can easily start a forest fire."

"What about the campfire we burned last night?"

"That was kept in a controlled environment."

"Oh, the hell with you guys, setting down the law. What makes you so superior anyhow?"

He suddenly lost interest in the argument, grinned, and said, "Do you have any food to spare? I already ate my lunch and am still hungry."

"We'll see if there's leftovers after we've eaten," I said. And to Tala, lowering my voice, "He acts like he smoked his joint already."

The Pacifico Mountain Campground was closed, so that we had the place to ourselves. We joined Jacob, Derek, Hannah, and London at the picnic tables and eagerly dug into the food we had carried up. Candie reached inside an outer pocket of Todd's backpack, pulled out Nick's bowl, and poured him a generous amount of water which he lapped noisily. Then he sat on his hinds, watching us eat, swallowing empty.

Tala asked, "Where's his lunch?"

"He only gets fed twice a day, morning and evening, but sometimes I give him a snack between meals," Candie replied. "And since he's been such a good boy on the way up, I'll give him one right now."

She turned to her pet and, stroking his head, went into baby talk, "Good doggie, Nicklausy! Mommy gives you a treatie." And she grabbed a dog biscuit out of Todd's bag.

Then she moved closer to me with a conspiratorial nod, saying, "I've been wanting to talk to you. They're going to make a movie of your book, *Stifle Her Scream*, right?"

"Where did you hear that?"

"Word gets around."

I said, "I'm in negotiations, but it's not a done deal yet."

Far from discouraged, she continued, "I'd be perfect for the lead part. When the time comes, put in a good word for me, will you, Sweetie?"

"If there should be a movie made from *Stifle Her Scream* - - and at this point that is undecided - - I doubt that I'd have any say about the casting."

She batted her eyes and insisted, "But you can try, Sweetie, can't you?"

I was spared from answering as Nick impatiently pulled at the leash and barked a couple of times, obviously needing to pee. Candie said, "Excuse us," and they walked off.

On the return hike we more or less stayed together in one group. We didn't need to preserve our breathing on the downhill stretches, so that there was ample chatter among us.

Jacob was reminiscing about Marcelo's hometown and shared some of his rock climbing experience in the Chilean Andes.

"Are you a climber?" he asked him.

"Not me, I'm afraid of heights," Marcelo replied.

Todd remarked, "The Andes sound awesome! Maybe one of these days I'll find the money to fly there and climb them."

Derek and Curtis trekked down a few paces ahead of me, and I saw Derek wrap an arm around his younger brother's shoulder. Looks like they've made peace, for the time being, I thought.

On some of the steep descents Candie had a hard time holding on to Nick, who would have preferred a free run down the slopes. She walked with a slight limp, an indication that despite the Band-Aid applied, the blister on her heel caused her discomfort.

Tala and Hannah found common ground for discussion in the medical field. From fragments of their conversation, I gathered that they debated medicating patients versus treating them with diet and natural remedies. London and I talked more shop, and before long, our group was back to where we had set up camp.

CHAPTER 12

At first, we did not see the Kim family upon return to our camp. I had an inkling of where they could be, walked to the edge of the plateau, and looked down the hillside. Sure enough, they were playing by the creek. Nick, who went unleashed at camp, had spotted them too and ran down to join in the fun. There was no doubt that Mikey and the dog had become best buddies.

When they came back up a while later, Mikey said, "I built this neat dam with rocks, and then Nicklaus jumped on top and destroyed it all."

Candie apologized for her dog's action, and the little boy petted Nick and said, "That's okay. I can build another one tomorrow."

Tired out but satisfied from the long hike, we relaxed for a while, took in the view, and were generally in a mellow mood. Hannah snapped pictures and Candie managed to be in most of them.

Then the actress went over to Derek and Curtis and asked, "So how big is your pawn shop?"

Derek replied, "The shop is family owned. There is Dad, me and Curtis, and about 20 employees."

"A good size," she said. "What kind of merchandise are you dealing with?"

"Anything; jewelry, antiques and collectables, old guns and tools, musical instruments. You name it, we buy, sell, and pawn the stuff. Depending on space available, we even take collectors' vehicles."

"That's good to know," she commented.

I was wondering whether Candie had a real interest or just made conversation.

Jacob had taken along a bocce ball set and some of us played backyard bocce. While traditional bocce is played on a court and players must keep their balls within the boundaries of that court, backyard bocce has no court or boundaries. We formed two four-person teams; Jacob, Hannah, London and Marcelo against Todd, Derek, Curtis and me. The Kims, Tala and Candie watched, the latter having a hard time keeping Nick out of the game.

We tossed a coin to determine who played first and our team got to start. Todd threw the small white ball, called the pallina, forward. He then tossed one of the colored bocce balls, trying to get it to stop as close to the pallina as possible. Then the play was switched to our opponents with Jacob trying to land his ball closer to the pallina than Todd's. He succeeded, and the play reverted to our team with Derek taking his turn. Derek's ball did not land closer to the pallina than Jacob's, and so it was up to Curtis to try bettering the point, which he did.

We continued in this fashion, with each team taking turns shooting until we had tossed all the bocce balls. Jacob's team won, with Hannah's ball being the closest to the pallina, beating my ball by one inch.

As Tala and I prepared the spaghetti and sauce dinner, the wind started to pick up, and it soon became clear that to light a campfire would be too dangerous. By the time the meal was over, the gusts had increased.

London said, "Feels like Santa Ana winds."

"You're right, but Santa Ana's are unusual this time of year. They happen more often in October," Todd commented.

We had eaten early, and Tala and I went to get water for doing the dishes before it got dark. When we returned from the creek, the group had gathered by the big tent, since we had no campfire. Jacob suggested singing camp songs. What we came up with sounded more like pirate or beer-drinking tunes. I looked over at the Kim family, who sat silent, and it was evident that they had never heard the melodies nor the lyrics.

I waited until we had finished the last verse of a hideous song and said to Min, "Tala and I enjoyed your singing last night. How about treating us to a solo?"

She was shy about it at first, but after we all begged, she gave in and asked, "What shall I sing?"

"Whatever you like. We'll be happy to listen to any of your songs," I replied.

She chose *Chanson Bohème* from the opera Carmen. Her soprano voice had a high vocal range any professional singer would have been proud of, and it rang clear and pure. We were elated to be given such a rare musical treat. When her melody ended with a crescendo, there was complete silence for a moment. Someone started clapping, and then we all applauded.

She bowed in a "thank you" gesture and then leaned close to her little boy, who whispered something in her ear.

Looking up at us, she said, "Mikey does not feel good. I think he's coming down with something." And so the Kim family retired for the night.

After such a wonderful performance, no one was in the mood to take up our own primitive singing again. We lingered a while longer, conversing in small groups of two or three. When the wind became even stronger, people decided to call it a night and headed for their respective tents.

As we walked to ours, Tala and I gazed at the stars above, and she remarked, "Look how bright they shine, more brilliant than I've ever seen in the city."

I pulled her close and said, "Like the meaning of your name, you're my brightest star!"

CHAPTER 13

In our tent, getting settled for the night, Tala remarked, "What an eventful day!" And after a pause, "I've got to hand it to Candie; she's resourceful. Bumming a shower from those people at the Monte Cristo Campground took finesse." She laughed and admitted, "Soon I'll feel cruddy enough to beg for a shower too since there is no way I can shampoo my hair for an entire week. You've got it easy. Just rubbing a wet washcloth over your close-cropped bristles will do."

She continued, "She sure was pushy when approaching you about getting her a part in *Stifle Her Scream.*"

"No kidding!"

"By the way, how *is* the movie deal coming along?"

"It is still a long time coming and may never happen. I get the feeling that there is squabbling going on within the movie makers' own ranks.

And where I come in, they want to make lots of changes, and they don't like the title."

"So?"

"What the hell! They can do anything they like with my story, as long as they cut me a fair price."

After a pause Tala remarked, "Tomorrow is Wednesday, so we've only been here two days, but it seems like a lot longer. By the end of the week we might get on each other's nerves."

"For some that already happened," I said. "Curtis, for one, is no longer a great fan of Jacob."

Then our talk touched on that day's hike. Tala commented, "We are a pretty fit bunch. For the guys belonging to the Sierra Mountaineering Club, the hike was like a stroll in the park, but I think the rest of us did a good job too. Even Candie showed serious wanderlust, blister and all."

I said, "I'm sure everyone knew what to expect from this trip or they wouldn't have signed up. And they all exercise in one way or another. Candie, for instance, might have never trekked up and down a mountain before, but judging by her firm body she must be working out on a regular basis. Marcelo rides his bike, Hannah and London are on a soccer team, and Yon and Min play tennis."

"How do you know all this?" my wife asked.

"I may not say much, but I keep my eyes and ears open."

"Spoken like a true writer," she teased.

I went on, "You keep in shape by doing Pilates, and I go on long neighborhood walks, which, considering the hilly area we live in, is more like hiking."

She giggled and said, "And the reason you prefer going on the walks alone is because your mind is full of plotting and you don't want to get distracted by my chatter."

"You are a dangerous woman. I can't keep any secrets from you!"

Getting back to our original subject I said, "Mikey is the only exception; the distance we covered was simply too much for his little legs and lungs."

"And don't forget Nicklaus. He kept up pretty good."

"He's got the advantage of an extra pair of legs," I pointed out.

"I wonder what we're going to do tomorrow."

"I'm sure there are many more hiking trails around, and if not, Jacob will think of something."

Tala remarked, "He sure is taking command."

"Bossing us around is what you mean," I said.

The windstorm gained in strength, and we could hear twigs and other debris being tossed about outside. Listening to the swirling noises, Tala said, "I'm sure glad we're tucked away safely in the tent."

Then she went back to her former train of thought and remarked, "Min has exceptional talent. I doubt that she's even aware that her voice is special." And in the next breath, "I hope Mikey hasn't caught anything serious and feels better in the morning. He sure is a sweet boy."

"Speaking of the kid, how about making our own?"

She slipped out of her sleeping bag and into mine, saying, "What are you waiting for? Let's get busy!"

CHAPTER 14

At two o'clock in the morning, we were rudely awoken by a loud blast, followed by continued howling of the wind. Our tent was fluttering dangerously, liable to break loose at any moment. Above the eerie sound of the gale, furious barking came from our left and the shrill sound of someone blowing the forest service safety whistle from the right.

A couple of minutes passed before I was fully conscious. Then I fumbled for the flashlight and cautiously opened the tent a crack, sticking my head out to assess the situation. Candie's tent had turned over and she and Nick were walking, or rather, being blown towards the road. The Kims' tent had disappeared, but Jacob's big dome was still standing. It was too dark to see anything farther away.

Todd came running and, trying to be heard over the roar of the wind, shouted, "People have taken refuge in our tent, but it isn't safe either. We're taking shelter in the cars."

I ducked back inside and said, "Our tent is going to blow. We'd better move."

Pointing the beam of the flashlight at Tala, I saw that she was already dressed and had pulled the hood of the windbreaker over her head. I quickly put on my pants and shoes, donned my hoodie, threw any loose articles I could find into our backpacks, and we were off.

The force of the elements hit with a vengeance as soon as we stepped out. It took all our strength to stay upright as we fought the wind every step of the way. I kept the flashlight pointing ahead, so that we could see obstacles on the ground. There was not much we could do about flying objects. Debris of any size was hurled all around us; from leaves, pine needles, and twigs, to uprooted chaparral shrubs. We just had to take the chance that nothing big or pointy would hit us.

When we were even with the dome tent, Jacob emerged, carrying Mikey, followed by Yon and Min. The walk to the cars was a battle, but we made it without injury or being swept away. All of us automatically stayed in the same grouping as on the drive up, and there was room in Jacob's van for Candie and Nick.

Soon after we settled into my SUV, it became clear that Mikey was indeed sick. Nobody had brought a thermometer along, but without a doubt, the boy was burning up with fever. Ever the nurse, Tala fished a container of Tylenol out of her bag.

Half delirious, the little boy asked, "Where is Nicklaus? Is he okay?"

I said, "I'm sure he's safe in the van. I'll check on him in a little while."

We learned later that the wind blew at 50 to 60 miles an hour, with occasional gusts reaching 90 miles an hour. At the time we did not know these numbers, just experienced the windstorm in its entire force of destruction. No wonder people called it California's evil wind.

It is a known fact that the hot, dry Santa Ana alters people's moods and increases angry or violent behavior. Given our circumstances, I was not surprised that tempers flared. When I entered the van to make sure everyone was accounted for and unharmed, a hot debate was in progress.

Candie was saying, "I'm sure everyone agrees that we should go home immediately. Some of our tents are gone, and even if we'd find them later, they'll be in shreds. My carry-on most likely went down the hillside too; I'm glad I left my other suitcases in the car."

Jacob stated, "Driving down the mountain road right now is reckless and out of the question. Vans and SUVs are especially vulnerable and could easily overturn. We have to wait until the wind dies down."

Hannah said, "That could take days! Our nerves are shot, and London and I just want to go home."

"Santa Ana winds are usually worse at night. Also, there may be debris on the road, which we couldn't see in the dark. We definitely need to wait until morning to make a decision."

"What decision?" Derek bellowed. "There is no decision to be made. We have to get out of here."

Jacob insisted, "It is perfectly safe inside the cars. Let's try to catch some sleep and we may look at the situation differently by daylight."

At that very moment there was a 90-miles-an hour gust, and seconds later we heard a tremendous bang coming from somewhere down the road. All were stunned, shaken to the core. Nick barked furiously, and when Candie calmed him down, the barking eased to a low whimpering.

Hannah said, "That sounded like a big car crash, or worse!"

"More like a train wreck," Derek put in.

Curtis glared at Jacob and said, "So much for your peaceful sleep!"

Todd, the logical one among us, stated, "There is nothing we can do at the moment; might as well try to get some rest." And he promptly leaned back in his seat and closed his eyes.

CHAPTER 15

I fought my way back to the SUV - - for every step forward, the wind hurled me half a step backward - - and found Mikey in worse shape. I reassured him that Nick was fine, but he didn't seem to understand or care. Tala had found rags in the glove compartment and used the tepid bottled water, left over from the previous night's dinner, to dip them in. She gently rubbed Mikey's forehead and chest, while Min did the same to his legs and feet.

I said, "I can try getting down to the creek to fetch cold water."

"Don't you dare!" Tala protested. "You'd get blown away before ever reaching it. Besides, this water here is perfect. Anything colder would be too much of a shock to his hot body."

Then she said, "The Tylenol isn't doing the trick; I can't get his fever down. I think he's got an ear infection and needs antibiotics."

I related the dispute that went down in the van. Marcelo was the only one listening. The women concentrated on taking care of Mikey, and Yon stared into space. I couldn't tell if he was praying, meditating, or had just tuned out.

Marcelo asked, "What was that loud boom we heard?"

"I have no idea. It came from farther down the road. A major crash or something must have occurred. It certainly freaked everyone out in the van. The sounds of the howling winds are bad enough, but that big bang scared the shit out of us."

Marcelo seemed calm and collected, but who knew what went on in that intelligent head of his. I had been half standing, half kneeling by the driver's seat, taking in the sad scene in my car. When I couldn't bear looking at the sick little boy, stretched out across his mom's and Tala's lap in the back seats, I turned toward the front and plopped into mine.

Marcelo, sitting next to me on the passenger side, said, "Todd is right. There is nothing we can do but wait. Wake me when we have a plan," and he closed his eyes.

I was jealous of Todd and Marcelo. They must have nerves of steel, I thought.

At dawn, I could stand it no longer and went out to pee. For the moment, the wind had diminished and I was able to walk steady. I got to the center of what used to be our campsite and stood still, overwhelmed by the widespread destruction. None of the four A-frame tents were standing where originally erected. Three were gone completely, and pieces of the fourth fluttered from a tree at the south end of the plateau. Jacob's dome tent was still there but had overturned and lay damaged on its side. All sorts of debris littered the area. I could not make out the campfire pit under all the rubble. Miraculously, the port-a-potty still stood, I presumed because it was sheltered by the bushes immediately in front of it.

On the way back, I tripped on something bulky sticking out of the ground underneath torn bush branches. Bending down and clearing the branches from the object, it became clear that I had stumbled on Candie's small bag. I picked it up and brought it along.

I was almost at the van when Candie stepped out, saying, "Come, Nicklaus. Jacob is being a jerk. We're outa here!" The dog jumped after her, and before she slammed the door, I heard Jacob say, "Good riddance!"

Then she saw me and said, "Oh, you found my carry-on. Thanks! Now I don't have to go home without makeup on."

"You're leaving?"

"You got it! I'm taking off before the wind kicks up again."

The woman wasn't kidding. As soon as she hit the Mercedes driver's seat, her fingers rummaged in her bag and out came the tools. Looking in the rearview mirror, she powdered her nose and applied mascara and lipstick. All this took only a few seconds. Then she maneuvered the vehicle out of her spot, waved, and drove off. I heard Nick's happy bark before the car rounded the first curve and then it was out of my sight. I turned my attention back to the van.

I had expected people to get ready to leave, but when I opened the door, I found myself in the midst of another heated argument.

Derek said, "Candie had the right idea bringing her own wheels." He shot Jacob a dirty look and added, "The rest of us are at your mercy."

Jacob said, "I admit, we may have to return home, but I'd like to check out the damage first and, if possible, salvage some of the tents. The windstorm isn't over by far; Candie acted irrationally. She should have waited until all are ready to leave. Caravanning down would have been safer."

Curtis shouted, "You idiot! Candie is the one who makes sense. Now is the time to get out of here before the wind kicks up again in full force."

Hannah said, "I'm sorry, Jacob, but at this point I really don't care if any of the tents are salvageable. We need to go home while we still can."

"Amen to that," Todd said.

London, who so far had not uttered a word and just sat there looking frightened, suddenly burst out, "This must be a nightmare and I'll wake up at any moment."

Hannah stroked her hand and said, "We'll be fine, Hon, I promise."

Jacob looked to me for help and pleaded, "Make them see reason, James."

I stated, "I have to side with the others. There is a sick little boy in my car who needs medical attention. We must leave and get down that mountain pronto."

Jacob threw up his arms in surrender and said, "Okay, majority rules."

CHAPTER 16

Jacob handed out bottled water and said, "How about breakfast?"

Nobody was in the mood to eat, so we got ready to leave. It only took a few minutes to disassemble the dome tent and place it inside the cargo trailer, and after everyone used the port-a-potty, it was also stowed away. Jacob searched the platform for the stove and grill, but gave up; they were either buried under the rubble or gone. Pushing the cargo trailer through the rubbish on the ground to where the van was parked took muscle, but with the combined effort of all the guys, we managed.

Jacob was about to hook the trailer to the van, when Candie and Nick came bustling up the road on foot. There was panic written all over Candie's face.

"What happened?" I asked.

Gasping for air, she stammered, "There's a huge uprooted tree blocking the road a little ways down." And she was close to hysteria when she added, "We're stuck up here!"

"Now we know what caused that big bang we heard in the middle of the night," Todd said.

Jacob asked, "Where's your car?"

"I left it there," she replied, still panting. "The tree is spread out across the entire width of the road, right after a curve. I came upon it suddenly and slammed on the brakes, coming to a halt right in front of the huge monster of a tree. I got scared and we hiked back up. It's only about a quarter mile down the road."

Curtis stated, "Like she said, we're stuck. Wouldn't it be nice to have a phone to call for help?" And pointing an accusing finger at Jacob, he yelled, "You got us into this mess; now get us out!"

Jacob's temper suddenly flared up and he shouted back, "Hey, we all agreed on the no gadgets rule before we came up, so don't blame me. I can't control the weather. I've about had it with your negative attitude. But don't worry, I'll get us out."

And after a pause he announced, "Okay, I'll go up to the forest service station for help."

True to his word, he drove off in the van within seconds. The rest of us tried to calm down and hoped he would succeed. We had all been outside when Candie came hiking back up and told us the bad news, except for Min and Tala, who stayed in the SUV tending to Mikey. I wasn't thrilled with the task, but I had to let them know about our latest setback.

Min did not seem to hear me or understand our dilemma. She was busy stroking Mikey's hair while gently talking to him in her language. Tala, on the other hand, was well aware of our grave situation.

She said, "Mikey's fever has gone down a bit, but his earache is worse. He really needs to see a doctor."

I could not look at the little guy twitching in agony any longer and said, "I'll let you know what's up as soon as Jacob is back," and left them again.

Fifteen minutes later, Hannah said, "What's keeping him? It can't take longer than two or three minutes to drive up and the same amount to drive back."

"He must be taking his sweet time and gabbing with the forest service guys," Candie said.

When Jacob finally returned, he was the bearer of more bad news. He had found the forest service station unmanned, which didn't make sense. When trekking past the station on our hike the day before, we'd seen people at work there. Considering the windstorm, one would expect the forest rangers to be on a keen lookout for forest fires.

Having no luck finding any humans at Mill Creek Summit, Jacob got the idea to continue driving down the other side of the mountain on Angeles Forest Highway toward Palmdale, hoping to get back to civilization and find help. He didn't get far. A couple of minutes into the ride, the road was blocked by rocks and large boulders, evidently caused by a recent rockslide.

With fallen rocks all over the road, he was left with no choice but to back the van up until he got to a turnout. This was a treacherous task, especially going around curves. It was a good thing that he had not hooked the trailer to his van yet, or it would have been even harder to maneuver. By the time he reached our campsite, he had broken into a cold sweat.

"Now what?" said Curtis.

Jacob looked beaten but said, "Don't anybody panic. We are minus the stove, but I have ready-to-eat food and water to last us several days."

Candie protested, "There is no way I'll stay up here another night. We need to get down today."

"I'm just saying, in the worst scenario we won't starve to death."

Marcelo spoke up for the first time and asked, "Do you have a plan B?"

"Of course, I do. I'll hike down to the Monte Cristo Campground. I'm sure the people who offered Candie their shower will have a phone. I'm also positive that they'll still be there. Driving down the mountain in a motorhome in windy weather is way too risky."

Jacob turned to Hannah and asked, "May I borrow your camera for a second?"

"Sure."

And while she went to fetch it from her backpack, Candie shouted, "I don't believe you!

Taking the time to snap pictures when we're in danger of our lives is the ultimate slap in the face."

"You bimbo! I need to document this for insurance purposes."

When handed the camera, he took a few shots of the destruction all around us, in particular of the area where the tents used to stand.

Giving the camera back to Hannah, he said, "I'll contact you once we're home if I need these photographs."

He gave us each a couple of energy bars, as well as an orange, and told us to help ourselves to more water if we liked. Then he packed his rucksack with his own ration of food and drink, plus a first-aid kit and windbreaker. He tucked the hunting knife and safety whistle into the pockets of his cargo pants.

Ready to go, he said, "It is approximately three miles to the Monte Cristo Campground, so it will take me about 45 minutes to get down and just over an hour to hike back up, plus a few minutes to talk with the folks and make the 911 call. I strongly advise you to stay put. The wind is likely going to intensify again at any moment."

He looked at his watch, stating, "It is 9:15. See you all no later than 11:15 to 11:30."

And to me he said, "You win the bet."

I wanted to tell him, I don't give a damn about the cursed bet, just get us out of here in one piece, but he had already turned his back on us and walked down the mountain.

CHAPTER 17

Severe hardship brings out the best or worst in people. In Tala and Min's case the former prevailed. For the rest of us the latter was true.

As soon as Jacob was out of sight, Curtis stepped a few paces away from the group and was about to light up.

Marcelo said, "Don't do that. It's dangerous!"

"I'll be careful."

Derek shouted, "You dumbass! Aren't we in enough shit already without you starting a fire?"

"There is nothing to do but wait around. Might as well have some fun."

"You moron! You're even dumber than I thought."

He flung himself at his brother, wrestling him to the ground, where they were caught in a fierce fistfight. The scuffle ended as fast as it had started, with Derek gaining the upper hand, managing to snatch the pot out of Curtis's hand.

Curtis got up on shaky legs, dusted himself off, rubbed his jaw that would soon swell up, and announced, "Now you all saw how violent my brother is!"

Todd said, "I don't know about your other disputes, but in this case Derek is right. There's still a steady breeze and it only takes one spark to start a forest fire. Your smoking would've put us all in jeopardy."

Curtis shouted, "What makes all of you think you're holier than Thou? I'm sick of it," and he stomped off down the hillside toward the creek.

Candie had recuperated from the initial shock of being trapped and was getting into a feisty mood of her own, saying, "What a pinheaded idea of Jacob's in the first place, picking a secluded spot when we could have stayed more comfortably at the Monte Cristo Campground."

Hannah shot back, "Let's not forget that the reason you came along was in the hope that your agent would arrange a publicity stunt! You must have planned to leave as soon as the paparazzi were through with you. So I'm sure you originally thought, the more rugged the place, the better for my "outdoorsy" new image. Now that things have taken a more serious turn, you've changed your opinion."

"You bitch! How arrogant can you get, assuming you know what I am thinking?"

Marcelo and Todd appeared to have an argument of their own, judging by Marcelo's hand gestures and Todd's shaking of his head. They stood by what used to be the campfire pit, so I was too far away to catch their words. My guess was that their bickering had something to do with Candie. After all, they had competed for her attention from the start.

London was tossing a stick in Nick's direction, trying to engage him in a throw-and-catch game, but it was no use. He just growled at her. Even the poodle felt the tension.

Then she looked at me and said, "When this is over, you'll have plenty of material for a new novel."

I snapped back, "It may never be over!" And walked away from her.

As our situation worsened, I blamed myself for the ordeal we were going through. If it had not been for suggesting that dumb bet to Jacob, we'd all be safe and sound at home and none of this would have happened.

Yon was pacing the length of our campsite, from where the cars were parked all the way to the end of the plateau and back. He seemed to be in his own personal hell. It must have been hard for a father to see his child suffer and be helpless to ease his pain.

I suddenly realized that I hadn't told Tala and Min about our newest complication.

CHAPTER 18

In the SUV, Min sang a tender lullaby to Mikey while Tala stroked his hand. The boy lay still with his eyes closed and seemed to be at peace for the moment. The three formed a serene picture, making me feel ashamed of the hostilities the rest of us had shown each other.

When Min's song came to an end, I gave them the latest report, ending with, "I'm sure we can expect help as soon as Jacob reaches the Monte Cristo Campground."

Tala asked, "Who went with him?"

"He hiked down alone."

"That's not a good idea with wild animals around. He said so himself, remember?"

I nodded.

"Well, go after him! If you hurry, you'll catch up."

She was right, of course. I grabbed my already packed backpack, threw her a kiss, and was on my way. I learned much later that I wasn't the only one disobeying Jacob's order to stay put. The rest of our group did likewise, except for Tala, Min, and the boy.

Jacob had about a ten-minute head start, and if I hustled, I might catch up with him. Did he go down the road or follow the creek? I asked myself. After a moment's hesitation I chose the road. The idea of an encounter with wild animals popped into my head, making me quicken my step to almost a run down the steep grade.

Soon, I came upon Candie's Mercedes, abandoned in front of a huge Jeffrey pine blocking the entire road. The tree stretched even beyond the road on both sides. There was a solid rock wall on the north side and a steep cliff on the south. Going around the tree on the upper side was out of the question; I wasn't prepared for rock climbing. Hiking down the bluff looked hazardous too, unless I backtracked a distance and went down the slope farther up the road. Another solution would be to climb across the fallen tree.

I wondered what Jacob had done at this point. Maybe it took him a long time to overcome the obstacle and he was still close by. Worth a try, I thought, and blew my whistle. I waited in vain for an answer from him, and then made the decision to tackle the Jeffrey pine. Just before I did, I thought I heard something or someone on the other side of the roadblock and called out, "Jacob! Is that you?" There was no answer.

I staggered, climbed, pulled along on all fours over the hurdle, getting whacked by branches, scratched by pine cones, and pricked by needles. Halfway through my task, I heard a sudden rustling sound coming from under a tree branch by my side. I stayed still, frozen with panic. There it was again, that swishing sound. This time I saw the rattlesnake pulling itself along a bough, not more than three feet from me. The snake slowly slithered away, but I didn't dare move for several minutes after I'd lost sight of the reptile. Jacob had warned us about rattlers, but faced with more pressing problems, I'd forgotten to look out for them.

When I finally emerged from the tree, my nerves were shot. Knees shaking and sweat pearls forming on my forehead, I needed to chill out. I sat down on the road a few paces from the fallen Jeffrey pine and blew the whistle once more, realizing that the act was useless. I wasn't going to catch up with Jacob.

Doubts and worries filled my head as I rushed down to the Monte Cristo Campground. One of my concerns was what I might find - - or not find - - when I got there. My anxiety grew with each step. What if the motorhome people and the other campers had already left? And if still there, what if they had no phone or their phone didn't get reception in the mountains? Where would we look for help, 30-some miles away from civilization, without transportation, and the winds apt to pick up again at any moment?

When I got to the access road of the campground, I sighed with relief when I saw the motorhome, parked in the same spot we'd glimpsed when passing by on our drive up. I thought, that was on Monday, and today is only Wednesday. It felt like we'd been trapped on this mountain for weeks! There was no trace of any tents, though. A couple of kids where playing by the stream that ran smack through the center of the campground. Otherwise, the place looked deserted.

I knocked at the RV's door, and when a man stuck his head out, I introduced myself and said, "Was my friend Jacob able to get through to 911, and is he still here?"

He stared at me.

"So he's on his way back up?"

The man said, "We didn't see anybody today other than our camping neighbors who abandoned their tent during the night and found refuge in our motorhome. A good thing too, since a few minutes later they lost it in the windstorm. They drove home early this morning when the wind died down. As you can see, we're the only ones left here."

CHAPTER 19

Thank God the man's cellphone worked and I got through to the authorities, telling all that had happened since the wind blew away our tents during the night. I stressed that we had a sick child who needed immediate medical attention. They already knew about the rockslide on Angeles Forest Highway near Mill Creek Summit, since the forest rangers had found the road impassable to their station early in the morning. They informed me that workers would be clearing away the boulders as soon as possible, and that the road was now closed to through traffic. However, the tree roadblock on the stretch of highway between our campsite and the Monte Cristo Campground was news to them.

There was a catch in my voice when I added, "And now it looks like my friend Jacob, the leader of our group, is missing," and I explained Jacob's circumstance. I mentioned that since I did not overtake him on my way down the road, he must have hiked along the creek but never reached the Monte Cristo Campground. I emphasized that I feared he could have had an accident and might be hurt. The dispatcher promised to send a helicopter to assess the situation and airlift people if necessary, and that the pilot would also keep an eye out for Jacob.

He said, "Sir, are you planning to stay at the Monte Cristo Campground?"

"No," I replied. "I'm hiking back up to the others and hope to find Jacob along the way."

"Be careful, sir!" And he added, "Should you hear or see the chopper above you, form an "X" with your arms, so that the navigator won't mistake you for your friend."

I ate my energy bars, drank some water, and then hiked back up, this time picking my way through the rugged terrain along the stream. I tried to focus on the strenuous task at hand, but couldn't help the unsettling pictures of Jacob's possible fate that crept into my mind. I replayed the best as well as the worst case scenario in my head. Stay positive, I told myself, over and over again.

In order to avoid uprooted small trees and bushes that lay at the bottom of the canyon, I had to turn away from the creek on occasion. At times, these detours led up steep slopes, and I caught myself panting, uncertain whether from exertion or anxiety. Every so often, I stood still for a moment with my eyes scanning the wilderness for any trace of Jacob. Except for an occasional splatter of the creek and the continued sound of a steady breeze wrestling with brush and tree branches, there was no movement or sound. I seemed to be the only human for miles.

About three quarters into the hike, I heard the helicopter. First, it flew behind me, following the course of the stream. Then it headed toward the road and circled approximately where the fallen Jeffrey pine blocked the highway. Next, it hovered over the cliff for a long moment. My heart beat faster as I wondered, is he finding Jacob?

The chopper looped around the road a few more times and then flew down the ravine straight at me. My first instinct was to duck as it stayed overhead, but then I remembered the instruction the 911 dispatcher gave and crossed my arms into the air in the shape of an "X". The pilot saluted and continued on toward our campsite.

My ordeal had taken a lot longer than Jacob's estimated two hours. In particular, the hike back up seemed to never end. When I reached our plateau, the time was past one o'clock in the afternoon.

CHAPTER 20

The first person I saw was London, and I asked, "Did Jacob come back, by any chance?"

"Isn't he with you?" she said, perplexed.

I shook my head.

"There was a helicopter circling above a little while ago, and we were sure Jacob had sent him to rescue us, but then it flew away."

"The pilot needed to appraise the situation first. He'll be back," I said.

Before long, everyone except for Min, who stayed in the SUV with Mikey, congregated around me and I told the shocking news. When I'd finished recounting the struggles of my last few hours, Tala, without uttering a word, ran into my arms, hugging me tight.

Todd asked, "So Jacob just vanished?"

"He may have had an accident," I said. "Hopefully the pilot in the chopper spotted him and a rescue team will be on the way."

Curtis said, "What about us?"

"Like I told London, the chopper will be back."

Tala took me aside and said, "I'm really worried about Mikey. He may permanently lose his hearing if not attended to." And she added, "Come, we have to reassure them that help is on the way."

It was heartbreaking to look at the little guy who lay across the backseat in agony. With as cheerful a tone I could muster, I asked, "Did you hear the helicopter?"

He nodded.

"You'll get to ride in it soon. Isn't that exciting?"

He tried to smile but could only manage a painful grimace.

To his mom I said, "They'll get him to a doctor without delay."

Minutes later, the chopper was back and kicked up dust and debris as it landed.

I asked the pilot, "Did you see our missing person?"

"No, I'm sorry." And he warned, "Mountain lions have been sighted in this area, so don't anyone wander off alone anymore."

The Kim family were the first to be airlifted and taken to the nearest emergency hospital. The helicopter made several more trips, taking the rest of the party to the Jock Master Sporting Goods parking lot.

Tala and I stayed behind to see if Jacob turned up, dead or alive. Todd offered to stay with me and let Tala go by helicopter, but she wouldn't hear of it.

By the time the Los Angeles County Search and Rescue Team arrived to look for Jacob, the wind had picked up again, making their job even harder. I wanted to help them search, but they wouldn't allow it. So there was nothing to do but wait. At dusk, they had to give up and continue the search the next morning.

Tala and I opened two cans of tuna, mixed the contents with mayo, and spread it on bread for dinner, followed by an apple each, washing it all down with water. We didn't have much of an appetite, but it was essential to keep up our energy level. We spent another night in the car, listening to the eerie sound of the destructive wind.

Early in the morning, we heard the chopper again and knew that the foot troops of the Los Angeles County Search and Rescue Team were also back at work.

Tala rubbed my back and said, "I wish I could ease your pain."

I said, "The longer it takes before they find him, the less chances are that he's alive."

"I know."

"And it's my fault."

She silently kept rubbing.

On Thursday afternoon, the team had extended their search to within a ten-mile radius of our campsite plateau, reaching far beyond both the Monte Cristo Campground and the Mill Creek

Summit. At nightfall, they had to throw in the towel. There simply was no trace of Jacob.

By the next morning, debris and boulders caused by the rockslide near Mill Creek Summit had been cleared away, and that stretch of the Angeles Forest Highway was re-opened. Removing the Jeffrey pine from the highway was still an ongoing project, requiring powerful machinery and more time. There had also been other damage to the highway farther down, so that its section toward Big Tujunga Canyon Road would stay closed for many more days.

With a heavy heart, Tala and I drove down the mountain toward Palmdale on Friday, April 5. The windstorm was over, but judging by the dark clouds in the sky, a rainstorm was brewing. Tala was behind the wheel of our SUV, and I drove Jacob's van. Candie's Mercedes was later being towed home. Jacob had given me his car keys before taking off on foot, just in case the van needed to be moved, he'd said. This made perfect sense at the time, but while driving in the direction of Palmdale on that miserable Friday, I mused, did he have a premonition?

CHAPTER 21

On Wednesday morning of the next week, Tala's day off, I sat in our den, the open laptop in front of me, staring at the one and only sentence I had written in an hour.

"It's no use, I'm a blockhead!" I yelled at the top of my voice.

Tala, still in her robe, came rushing over and asked, "Are you okay?"

"Sure, just frustrated as hell. I can't concentrate."

"When's your deadline for handing the book to the publisher?"

"December 13."

"Relax, you've got plenty of time."

"That's what you think!"

She gave me a playful shove and said, "A change of scenery might help. I have no big plans for the day, and cleaning the house can wait. So let's go somewhere."

I thought about it, and then replied, "I've been meaning to go on a research trip. Want to come along?"

"Where to?"

"Oh, not far. Just Downtown Los Angeles."

"I haven't been Downtown in ages. Let's go by train."

And so we boarded it within the next hour in Pasadena, taking the Metro Gold Line.

The majority of people on the train were texting or playing with their smartphones. Even a toddler was scrolling and punching on his make-believe version. The rest had either fallen asleep or stared into space, oblivious to their surroundings. Tala and I were the only ones looking out the window. The train ride had little to do with "rapid transit" and was certainly no "express," as it stopped at every station. We were in no hurry and did not mind. As we approached our destination of Union Station, I noticed that the L.A. River was almost dry with only a trickle of a water flow.

As we got off the train and platform, making our way over to the main building, Tala asked, "Where, exactly, do we go for your research?"

"I need to check something out in the jewelry district, but if you like, I'll show you some of L.A.'s sights first."

"I likes," she said in broken English, obviously messing with me.

I had been to Union Station many times before and knew some of its history, but Tala seldom had occasion to go there.

We walked through the waiting room, a reminder of a bygone era. It had walls of travertine marble and acoustical tile, a terra cotta tile floor with a central strip of inlaid marble, leather chairs with carved wood armrests, and a high glass ceiling.

Tala remarked, "I'd forgotten what a gorgeous, classy place this was. I can picture what it must have been like a century ago, with people dressed in their finest when traveling by train."

"Not quite a century," I corrected. "Union Station only opened in 1939. It served trains from the Union Pacific, Santa Fe, and Southern Pacific Railways, and is a historic landmark. Over the years, several movies have been shot here."

We exited the station at Alameda and walked over to Olvera Street, a toast to old Mexico. The area was a major tourist attraction and extremely successful, thanks to its authenticity and preservation of Hispanic culture. We walked along small vendor stands, flanked by restaurants. Vendors sold piñatas, sombreros, serapes, Mexican pottery, leather goods, traditional Mexican dresses, and all kinds of souvenirs.

As we passed by one of the many eateries with outdoor seating, I asked, "Are you hungry yet?"

"It's way too early; I couldn't eat a bite."

We headed north on Broadway and walked under the golden dragon gateway that marked the entrance to Chinatown. Compared with other major cities, the Los Angeles Chinatown was relatively small. It consisted of dozens of restaurants, herbal shops, bakeries and souvenir stores. We passed a market with its doors open and inhaled the smells of exotic foods. At the Central Plaza, the most popular tourist attractions seemed to be the wishing well and a statue of Bruce Lee.

We turned back south again, walked along Broadway, and briefly watched the traffic from the overpass of the 101 Freeway. Then we trekked uphill on Temple Street to the Cathedral of Our Lady of the Angels. The cathedral has a postmodern architecture, and a contemporary style dominates the interior.

As we passed through the bronze doors and the statue called *The Virgin Mary*, Tala remarked, "This modern depiction of the *Virgin* is a far cry from any of the images I've ever seen of her!"

Once inside, Tala went straight to a pew and knelt down in prayer, while I walked along the walls of the nave and studied the tapestry hangings of the *Communion of Saints*. On the wall by the baptismal font was another enormous tapestry work depicting Jesus being baptized by John the Baptist in the River Jordan. I didn't know anything about organs but was duly impressed with the colossal pipes of the Dobson organ. Then I joined Tala at the life-size bronze crucifix behind the altar, which was extremely realistic and awe inspiring.

We descended the stairs to the mausoleum in the lower level. It contained crypts and niches for burials. Many past bishops and cardinals were memorialized in the mausoleum, as well as laity, among them June Marlowe and Gregory Peck. Tala seemed impressed with the numerous stained glass windows and studied each one.

Once back in the open air, we continued south on Hill Street, getting a good view of imposing City Hall to our left, and passed several court buildings. We walked among tourists, the homeless, and lawyers in three-piece suits, pulling their documents along in dollies. We stood at the bottom of Angels Flight, the funicular dating back to 1901, when Bunker Hill was a fashionable neighborhood. The incline railway cars were not in operation, though. Then we crossed the street and entered the Grand Central Market.

Inside the market, one can buy fresh vegetables and fruits, imported cheeses, meats, fish, pastries, and liquor, among other delicacies. We also passed plenty of eateries. We had entered the market on Hill Street and exited it on Broadway. We kept walking south on Broadway, lined with one bridal store after another.

Just before reaching 7th Street, I pointed across the street and said, "Over there used to be Clifton's Cafeteria, an L.A. landmark. It has been closed for renovations for years. I'm starting to doubt that it will ever re-open."

At this point we got into the jewelry district and turned right into 7th Street. Tala glanced into a side alley where a row of adjoining buildings resembled neighborhoods one would encounter in European towns. The ground floors consisted of restaurants and cafes, and the second stories might have been apartments or housed the restaurant owners.

"How cute!" she exclaimed, pointing up at one of the building's second story, which sported a diminutive balcony facade with potted geraniums along the railing.

"Feel like having lunch here?" I asked.

She shook her head. "I'm not hungry yet."

"In that case, let's get to the main purpose of this outing," I said.

CHAPTER 22

The entire area was abundant with jewelry retail stores, stretching over several blocks, some in sizable merchant buildings, with individual stall spaces rented out to jewelry dealers. I chose one of the larger buildings and we went inside. The immense quantity of sparkling gold, silver, diamond, and other precious stone jewelry pieces displayed by so many merchants, all under one roof, was blinding.

Tala sucked in her breath and said, "I'm getting dizzy from all the glitz."

We browsed for a few minutes, going from stall to stall, glancing into the glass display counters, and she asked, "So what is it you're researching?"

"Shush, I'll tell you later," I replied.

We kept up the perusing, and when Tala came to a halt in front of one of the stations, glancing intently into a showcase which displayed rows of sparkling earrings, I said, "Pick out something."

"What are you saying?"

"Make a choice. Within reason, that is."

"You're buying me jewelry?"

Instead of an answer, I grinned at her.

The dealer behind the counter was quick to react and said, "The lady is interested in earrings? What can I show you?"

Tala pointed to a pair of hoop earrings and asked, "Are these white gold?"

"All of my jewelry is gold. I don't sell silver."

He unlocked the glass counter case with a key, pushed the sliding door aside, grasped the earrings Tala had indicated, and placed them on a black velvet cushion on top of the counter for her to admire. While doing so he said, "These are solid 14-karat white gold diamond-cut etched. You have good taste!"

Tala picked them up and after a lengthy scrutiny announced, "They're gorgeous!"

She gave me the look and continued "You know, of course, that I have yellow gold hoops, but I've always wanted white gold ones."

I asked the merchant, "What's your price?"

"$295."

My practical Tala said, "With tax added it comes to over $320. That's more than we're willing to spend." And turning to me, she said, "Thanks for the thought."

Even though Tala seemed to have lost interest, I glanced at the rows of earrings inside the case and asked the guy, "Are any of these less expensive?"

"Sure," he said. "Which ones are you interested in?"

Tala pointed out several others, which the dealer took out, one at a time. Most were in the low $200 range.

I am no expert, but could tell that the very first pair she had picked out was by far the nicest. I said, "You had your heart set on the diamond-cut pair, and so be it. Consider it an early Christmas present."

The merchant beamed and stated, "For you, I lower the price to $280."

Out on the street, Tala kissed me and said, "Thank you for the wonderful Christmas present. My first ever received in April!"

We had walked half a block before she exclaimed, "Oh, you forgot about your research. Let's go back."

She was halfway turned around when I stated, "The research is over and done with. Unfortunately, what I had in mind for my story won't work. I'll have to think of something else."

"I don't understand."

I explained, "Did you notice that the jeweler opened the sliding display glass case with a key and locked it again each time he took out a pair of earrings?"

"No, I didn't. Guess I was preoccupied with checking out the earrings."

"Well, I paid attention. He never left it open. We had him show us six pairs of earrings, and he never left more than one pair on the counter at the same time. He opened and relocked the case each time he took out an item. Even when I distracted him with questions, he didn't fail to lock up after each transaction."

"I don't get what you're driving at."

I said, "Never mind. My experiment didn't work. I was hoping by creating a diversion it might be possible to distract the dealer and he would leave the case open long enough for a thief to make a switch of merchandise. That would never happen. The guy opened and relocked his showcase like a programmed robot. I needed to come here to check out if my idea would be possible. Now I know that it isn't. I'll have to go back to the drawing board."

Then I suggested, "We could head over to the garment district. Do you need any clothes?"

"No point in overdoing it," she replied. "I'm more than happy with the jewelry you just bought me!"

On the way back to Union Station we took 3rd Street and happened upon Little Tokyo. At the entrance of Japanese Village Plaza is the Little Tokyo's Watchtower, a replica of a rural Japanese fire lookout tower. We also passed the Friendship Knot sculpture. The plaza is a small area of shops and restaurants with colorful paper lanterns strung overhead. We walked the short distance over to the center of Little Tokyo to Weller Court, where we found more shops offering Japanese imports, restaurants, and bakeries.

Dying of thirst, we went inside the Marukai Supermarket, which specialized in Japanese specialty foods and offered a large collection of Japanese beauty products. We purchased two bottles of water and then made our way to Alameda Street, the road that would bring us back to the train station.

Walking along it, Tala pointed ahead and remarked, "What a strange looking building with nothing but vertical slots for windows."

"That's the Metropolitan Detention Center," I said.

"Oh, a prison. Makes sense."

"It's not actually a prison, just a holding jail."

By the time we finally stood in front of Union Station, we were starved.

Tala asked, "There is food in there, right?"

"Yes, but I have a better idea. Let's lunch at Philippe's, just a short distance farther up Alameda."

Philippe's was one of the oldest restaurants in Los Angeles, a traditional delicatessen type, famous for their French dip sandwiches. There was a rustic feeling about the place, with dark wood for walls and sawdust scattered on the floor. We ordered our French dips and freshly brewed iced teas at the counter, and then carried food and drinks to one of the large communal tables we shared with strangers.

Later, getting off the train in Pasadena and walking to where our car was parked, Tala said, "I had a great time today!"

"Me too," I agreed. "And the thought of Jacob's fate never entered my mind all day."

CHAPTER 23

For the next six months, the familiar routines of everyday life helped to steady our emotions, giving us back a sense of normalcy. It was easier for Tala. The job at the hospital required her full attention. There was no time for brooding. I wasn't that lucky. Although I tried with all my might to immerse myself into my current manuscript, more often than not, I caught myself staring into space, re-living our disastrous camping trip.

Tala kept in touch with Min and fortunately, after receiving antibiotic treatment, Mikey had recovered within a few days and suffered no permanent hearing loss. Hannah called to make sure we got home okay, and Candie had the nerve to pump me again about getting the lead role in the *Stifle Her Scream* movie. We didn't hear from any of the others.

The official status on Jacob's police report was classified as a "missing person."

At first, we all hoped that he was still alive and would turn up. On being notified, his parents flew in from Florida and stayed in Southern California in order to be close by, should there be news of him. After a month passed, even his parents had to come to terms with the fact that, if their son would ever be found, he'd most likely be dead. Defeated, they returned home.

The speculations of Jacob's fate included everything from being killed and eaten by wild animals or murdered in cold blood to having been abducted by aliens. People in general agreed logic dictated that if Jacob had accidentally fallen down the cliff, the mountain rescue team would have found him, dead or alive.

One evening, soon after Jacob's disappearance, Tala said, "It must be hard on Holly. Shall we have her over for dinner one day?"

"What would we talk about?" I objected. "The four of us spent so many fun evenings that getting together without Jacob might be awkward and only cause her more pain. It was bad enough having to face her when returning his van."

"Guess you're right."

And after a pause she asked, "How long have we known Jacob?"

"Let me think. It was nine years ago when chance threw us together to serve on that jury. He was straight out of college and looking for a job when he got the summons, and I had just published my second book and needed to promote it. We were both pissed off at not having been smart enough to figure out a way to be excused."

"I remember! You were in a foul mood for days until you finally decided you might as well enjoy the ride."

"The ride was six weeks long. We thought the trial would never end."

"And then you brought him home one night and became the best of buddies." She sighed and continued, "And how long has it been since Holly got into the picture, three years?"

"More like four," I corrected.

Tala sighed again and stated, "No wonder there's a big void in our lives."

CHAPTER 24

In September, when local media reported that hikers had stumbled on human remains near Crystal Lake in the San Gabriel Mountains, none of us linked the information to Jacob. The Crystal Lake area was about 30 miles east of where our group had set camp in April.

We were therefore stunned to learn in October that the cadaver found in the Crystal Lake area was identified as that of Jacob. Positive DNA evidence showed the advanced decomposed human remains were Jacob's. There was no disputing DNA proof, but how was it possible that he went missing on foot near the Monte Cristo Campground and ended up being found dead at Crystal Lake?

One theory went that he was carried off to a mountain lion's den, another that he got lost and hiked east, instead of following the road or the creek. Yet another, that he was murdered at the

Monte Cristo Campsite by the motorhome people, then driven to Crystal Lake and dumped.

None of these scenarios made any sense. Wild animals do carry off their prey, but 30 miles is a bit farfetched. The notion that Jacob got lost was ridiculous. He knew the area better than most. And what motive would the motorhome folks - - complete strangers - - have for killing him?

Tala and I discussed it at length, but were clueless as to what fate Jacob could have possibly met, having gone missing near our campsite and turning up dead some 30 miles farther east, six months later. We could only hope that, no matter what happened, he went fast and did not suffer.

In any event, his parents made the trip to California once more and later returned to Florida with their son's ashes, where they held a memorial service among friends and relatives. I doubt that they had closure, since the circumstances of his death were still a mystery.

We had talked to the authorities back in April when filing a missing person's report. With the identification of Jacob's remains in October, an in-depth investigation was indicated, so the call from the Los Angeles County Sheriff's Department came as no surprise. The appointment for our interview was scheduled for Wednesday, October 9, on Tala's day off.

CHAPTER 25

Two plain-clothed officers showed up at our home on that Wednesday, and they introduced themselves as Lieutenant Yager and Deputy Sheriff Knox. The lieutenant, a stocky middle-aged man, was in charge. We sat down in the den, and he asked if we were fine with the interview being recorded. Having no objection, we watched as the tall, lean deputy set up the recording device. Lieutenant Yager began by re-hashing our personal information while his subordinate took notes. Then he got to the gist of the matter.

He had me repeat my account, step by step, of what happened after I left the camping plateau on foot, chasing after Jacob. Recalling the event in detail was easy; I'd re-lived the ordeal in my mind numerous times in the six months from April to October. Even today, over eight years later, the incident is forever stamped into my brain. The lieutenant heard me out, never interrupting.

At the end of my long statement he said, "Now, Mr. Eaton, I am going to ask you a few important questions. How long after Jacob Barrstein did you take off toward the Monte Cristo Campground?"

I replied, "About 10 minutes, 15 tops."

"Are you sure? It's important."

"Positive."

"Did others in the group walk away from your campsite?"

I hesitated and then admitted, "We all got testy with one another after Jacob took off. Curtis got into a fight with his brother and then left, sulking."

"In which direction?"

"Downward, to the creek."

"Did anyone else leave?"

"I don't know," I replied.

Tala commented, "Todd and Marcelo took off a bit later."

"Do you know why?" the lieutenant asked.

"Min and I were taking care of Mikey, and Marcelo stepped inside our SUV to get his jacket. He told us that he and Todd were going to check what was going on. We had heard a safety whistle being blown."

"That must have been me," I put in.

Tala continued, "They went as far as Candie's car, then turned back. They told us later that they hadn't seen anyone."

Lieutenant Yager nodded, then scratched his head and said, "By the way, what was the reason you folks picked that particular area to pitch your tents and not a public campground?"

He left me no choice; I had to tell about the bet.

"I see," he said. "How much was it for?"

I felt silly when answering, "A thousand dollars."

"That's a substantial sum as far as friendly bets go. Peanuts to a bestseller author, though."

I was tempted to point out the enormous amount of effort, time, and money spent on promoting a book but let it slide. Instead I simply said, "I wish we'd never made the bet."

"I understand from the missing person report filed in April that you and Mr. Barrstein were good friends. How long was that friendship?"

"I've known Jacob for nine years."

The lieutenant turned to Tala and asked, "Would you like to be called Ms. or Mrs. Eaton?"

"Either is fine."

"So Ms. Eaton, where were you while your husband hiked to Monte Cristo and back?"

"I was in the SUV with Min and Mikey."

"The entire time?"

"I left twice. The first time I needed to urinate, and the second was when the helicopter circled around the area and I assumed we were being rescued."

"You mentioned that two people, I believe you said Todd and Marcelo, wandered off. So far we've established that Jacob, your husband, Curtis, Todd, and Marcelo left the campsite. Did everyone else stay put?"

"I don't know. Min and I took care of her sick little boy, and I honestly didn't pay attention to what went on outside the SUV."

"No matter. We'll soon interview the others concerned and learn about each person's movements in due time."

He motioned to Deputy Knox, who reached into his briefcase and pulled out a plastic evidence bag and then handed it over to his superior.

Lieutenant Yager held it in front of my eyes, saying, "You recognize this?"

I gasped and stared at the object visible through the transparent evidence bag and said, "Yes, I do. That's Jacob's hunting knife. Was it found on Jacob at Crystal Lake?"

"No, road workers hit upon it when clearing away the tree which blocked the road on Angeles Forest Highway. They found the knife on the bluff, south of the highway."

"So he *did* take the road and didn't follow the stream, after all," I said.

"It certainly looks that way."

After a pause I asked, "Had the knife been used?"

He smiled and replied, "You are applying your brain, I see. Must be the mystery writer detective in you! To answer your question, the knife was clean with no traces of blood on it."

I said, "It was treacherous climbing over that Jeffrey pine; I had to crawl on all fours at times. Still, I don't believe Jacob lost the knife out of the pocket of his pants. He was a careful man."

The lieutenant nodded and agreed, "I don't believe it either."

"So what does it mean?"

"There could have been a struggle, say, with a mountain lion or another human being, and he pulled his knife but never got the chance to use it."

I thought about this for a second and then argued, "Wouldn't the road workers have found blood, Jacob's blood, in the area?"

"Not likely. It rained for several days. That was one of the reasons the removal of the tree took so long. First the windstorm, then the downpour."

Tala couldn't take it any longer and said, "Please, do we have to discuss the gory details?"

I squeezed her hand and gave her an apologetic look, while Lieutenant Yager remarked, "Sorry, Ms. Eaton, but being a nurse, you must be used to blood."

"Sure, but it isn't every day that I picture someone being mauled by a mountain lion."

I said, "How did he end up at Crystal Lake?"

"He could have been dragged to the animal's den."

"30 miles?"

Lieutenant Yager stated, "You are correct. Crystal Lake is approximately 30 road-miles away from where your group had set up camp, but the distance is only 16 miles when cutting straight through the woods. Wild cats can carry their prey that far."

"Prey the size of a human being?" I asked.

"Yes, but not necessarily all in one piece. And it may have taken the animal several days to make the transport."

I heard Tala take in her breath. For my part, I refused to visualize that concept.

After a pause I asked, "So you assume a wild animal was the killer?"

"There is no evidence of that, but we're not ruling it out at this point," the lieutenant replied. "There are numerous possibilities. For instance, he could have fallen off the cliff, broken his neck, and then been carried off by animals, which would make his death accidental. Or, a human could have taken his life, and in that case it would be a homicide. It is simply too early to tell. That is why we're conducting the investigation."

He turned back to Tala and said, "By the way, Ms. Eaton, how long did *you* know Mr. Barrstein?"

"Also nine years," she replied.

There wasn't anything left to discuss. Lieutenant Yager thanked us for our time, the deputy stuffed the evidence bag, his notes, and the recording device back into his briefcase, and I showed the two officers to the door.

After they had left, it occurred to me that Deputy Sheriff Knox had not opened his mouth once during the entire interview.

CHAPTER 26

At dinner that evening, Tala said, "That wisecrack the lieutenant made about you being a bestselling author was uncalled for."

"In a way it was a compliment, considering I was only on the bestseller list for one month."

Then she asked, "Do you really believe the mountain lion theory?"

"It could have happened, but I doubt that it can be proven."

She shuddered and said, "It's a horrible idea; I don't want to picture it. And aside from Jacob falling down the cliff by accident, every other solution is equally disturbing."

I nodded and said, "It would mean that a person in the camping group could be a murderer. Not a pleasant thought."

"Will we ever know the truth?"

"Maybe not, but let's give Lieutenant Yager a chance."

"Do you think that he knows more than what he told us?"

"Of course he does."

We ate the rest of the meal in silence, each pre-occupied with our own private thoughts.

When clearing the table I said, "I have some good news. I've sold the movie option rights to my book. They're hiring people to get the screenplay written as we speak. I probably won't recognize my story when they're through with it, but who cares!"

"Does that mean you have a contract?"

"Yep."

"Congratulations! Let's open the bottle of champagne we've had ready in the fridge for weeks to celebrate this occasion."

I popped it open and filled our glasses. We clinked them, and I held mine up in a toast, "To the success of the movie *Stifle Her Scream* or whatever the hell they're going to name it!"

"Hear, hear!" Tala said, and raised hers.

Then she giggled and asked, "Are we rich?"

I laughed too and answered, "For now, I'm only getting a small advance. As for later, who knows what will develop?"

Tala suddenly got serious and said, "I almost forgot to tell you. Min called today and suggested a group get-together in Jacob's honor."

"You mean a memorial service?"

"Nothing formal. Just a gathering of the April camping crowd."

"That's not a bad idea since we didn't fly to his memorial service in Florida. Where are we going to have it?"

"Min offered to invite everyone to her house. She asked me for people's phone numbers. Do we have them?"

"I saved the list Jacob sent in a Word file at the time we planned the trip."

CHAPTER 27

A couple of days later, Candie's agent e-mailed me with an official request to have me recommend her for the lead role in the movie adaption of my book. How did he hear of my contract so fast? I wondered. These Hollywood people must be equipped with radar!

When I told Tala, she asked, "So how did you answer the agent?"

"That it was out of my hands and he should get in touch with the producer."

"Is that true?"

"What?"

"You have no say in the casting and couldn't put in a good word for Candie?"

I shrugged and said, "Maybe I could. I don't have a clue how the intricate wheels of the movie industry turn."

"But you don't like her and won't try?"

"Not liking her has nothing to do with it. She isn't right for the part."

That said, we dropped the subject. The truth was that I modeled the main character in the story after my wife. Tala had read the book but didn't recognize herself in the character and I liked to keep it that way. Besides being an olive-complexioned beauty, the woman in the book was smart, serene, down-to-earth, and brave. Having her turned into a blonde airhead in the movie would be hard for me to swallow.

Tala clued me in on another matter and said, "About the gathering in Jacob's honor. Between Min and me, we were able to get a hold of people. We're planning it for next Tuesday evening, October 15, at 7:30. Min wanted to have it earlier and serve dinner, but I told her that would be way too much trouble, since we're a dozen people."

"So all are coming?" I asked.

"Yes, everyone has committed to it." And she added, "By the way, I told Holly about the get-together and she wants to come."

"Why? Didn't she already attend the memorial service in Florida?"

"Sure she did, but she'd like to talk to people who spent the last couple of days with Jacob before he disappeared."

"Is that a good idea? Speaking to the campers and learning the details of our windstorm ordeal, and what it led to, may be more upsetting to her than helpful."

"I agree, but she insists on coming. And you know Holly. Once she has set her mind on something, nobody can talk her out of it."

CHAPTER 28

We brought Holly along and arrived at the Kims' residence a few minutes early. Yon and Mikey greeted us at the door, then showed us to the living room. It was evident that Yon and Min were used to entertaining. A sofa, love seat, and a couple of upholstered chairs stood grouped around a Steinway Grand Piano. Yon was in the process of bringing extra chairs from the adjacent dining room where Min placed platters stacked with food on the table.

We introduced them to Holly. Min touched her arm and said, "I am so sorry about Jacob."

As far as I could tell, Min's compassion rang true and Holly seemed touched, and to overcome her emotion she quickly turned to the boy and said, "So you are Mikey. That is one of my favorite names."

Tala addressed Min and said, "You weren't supposed to cook!"

"Oh, these are just some snacks and a dessert," Min said, gesturing with her hands, indicating that the dishes were nothing special.

Pointing to rows of rolled-up refreshments, Tala asked, "What are those?"

"That's *gimbap*, made of steamed white rice, seasoned meat and vegetables rolled in dried seaweed."

"What are the things in the dish you just put on the table?"

"Those are *Mandu*, which are Korean dumplings. I filled them with minced meat."

"May I try one?" I asked.

"Of course, they're here to eat. Dip it in the sauce."

I helped myself to a dumpling, which was delicious.

We learned that *maejakgwa*, the dessert she had also set on the table, was made from ginger, cinnamon, and pine nuts.

The rest of our ill-fated April camping group came trickling in. Some showed surprise and seemed uncomfortable when introduced to Jacob's girlfriend, and others appeared indifferent to the fact. By the time all were present, it was past eight o'clock. Disappointment registered all over Mikey's small face when Candie showed up alone.

"Where's Nicklaus?" he wanted to know.

"Sorry, he couldn't come as it's his bedtime soon."

Min said, "That reminds me; it's past *your* bedtime, Mikey. Remember, we said you could stay up to say hello, but now you need to go upstairs and get ready for bed. I'll come up in a few minutes."

He obediently said good-night and then hurried up the steps.

Tala turned to Hannah and London and asked, "Are congratulations in order?"

"Yes," they said in unison. "We got married June 8."

Everyone followed suit with good wishes for the pair.

Addressing her guests, Min said, "Please get comfortable and help yourselves to snacks. There is tea and coffee set out, and if you prefer juice or water, I'll get it for you."

And so we got settled. Candie chose the sofa, and it came as no surprise that Todd and Marcelo plopped down on either side of her. As far as conversations went, people seemed ill at ease, understandably so, considering this was the first time we had seen one another since our tragic experience six months earlier.

I was trying to think of something clever to say when Min came back down the stairs from tucking Mikey in, sat down at the piano and announced, "If it's okay with everyone, I'd like to sing a gospel in Jacob's honor."

And without further ado, she played and sang *Go tell it on the Mountain*. We knew that she mastered opera, and now she did the African-American spiritual song equal justice. Considering the reason we were assembled, the melody and lyrics were gripping. Several of us had moist eyes as Min finished the last refrain.

There followed a long silence, and then I said, "As you all know, Jacob was a longtime friend of mine, and we shared many good times. But the memory of him that sticks in my mind most is sitting in that jury deliberation room together. He convinced the rest of us jurors that his take on the case was the only correct one. He was right, and it was thanks to him that we handed over a just verdict."

I ended with, "Would any of you like to add a token in his remembrance?"

A couple of people shared some qualities they had admired in Jacob; his leadership, common sense, and endurance of hardship.

Curtis suddenly blurted, "We're not supposed to put down the dead, but I'm not going to be a hypocrite. Jacob was a bossy SOB."

Derek commented, "You think that everyone in authority is bossy, but in Jacob's case you're right. He was a damn tyrant."

I looked over at Holly and saw shock in her face, but she bit her tongue and said nothing.

Todd spoke up. "Someone has to take charge with a group of campers. Otherwise there would be chaos. Jacob had the skills, so I was fine with him being in charge. He overreacted, though, about Candie's smartphone. That was uncalled for."

Holly asked, "What happened with Candie's phone?"

Candie took over and gave a dramatic account of the episode. Other folks would have just stated that Jacob threw her phone down the mountain, but Candie re-enacted the entire scene, dialogue and all. I had to admit to myself that she may be a better actress than I had given her credit for.

Holly, who always reminded me of a cat - - green-eyed, independent, and alert - - said, "Would anyone please fill me in on what exactly happened up on that mountain? I'd like to get as close as possible a look into Jacob's last two camping days."

Marcelo took the role of storyteller, and in his precise scholarly English went over the events from the time we first set up camp to the devastating windstorm that blew away our tents in the middle of the night, ending with Jacob seeking help at the Monte Cristo Campground. Here and there, the rest of us added minor facts he'd left out.

When he'd finished, Hannah said, "Looking back, Jacob held up well under pressure. The rest of us were not as level headed. And we were not exactly kind to him on that last day, remember?"

We all nodded.

Marcelo stated, "Never forget, he died while attempting to get help for us all."

CHAPTER 29

We were sampling Min's dessert of *maejakgwa*. The crunchy ginger cookies made a crackling sound with each bite. Min was a gracious hostess and as all relaxed, the gathering took on a more lighthearted side. Conversations ranged from current events, sports and the latest movies, to Hannah and London's recent wedding celebration.

Then Yon made us all aware again of the reason we were there by saying, "Two officers from the Sheriff's Department came to take our statements yesterday. Did they interview any of you?"

"I had the pleasure too," London said, sarcastically.

I stated, "Lieutenant Yager and Deputy Sheriff Knox also paid Tala and me a visit last week, and I'm sure they'll talk to the rest of you soon."

Derek asked, "What did they want to know?"

"Among other things, they were interested in everyone's whereabouts at the crucial time after

Jacob took off in the direction of the Monte Cristo Campground. Of course I could only speak for myself." Looking at Curtis, I added, "I did tell them, though, that you got into a fight with your brother, taking off in anger soon after Jacob left."

"Thanks a lot!"

"It stands to reason that the lieutenant would have learned that fact sooner or later. It was best to hold nothing back."

Todd said, "So are we suspects?"

"That is usually the case in an investigation," Marcelo put in. And he suggested, "We should synchronize our movements. Might as well start with you, Curtis. So where did you go after the fight with your brother?"

"None of your damn business!"

"Maybe not, but the police will make it their business."

Curtis shrugged and said, "Okay, I'll tell you. I've got nothing to hide. I was mad as hell at all of you and needed some down time. First I hiked down to the creek. When I got there, I'd cooled down some but didn't feel like facing any of you guys yet. I got the idea to cut across the gulch and trek to the highway to see the tree that blocked the road for myself. Maybe Candie had exaggerated and there was a way to pass through. I got to about 20 yards from the highway when I saw James coming around a bend. I didn't want to talk to him and ducked behind a bush."

He looked my way and said, "You didn't see me, and after you passed by, I changed my mind about heading toward the tree. Once on the road, I hiked up, in the opposite direction. When even with the van and SUV, I still didn't want to talk to anybody and just kept on going. At one point, I thought I heard a whistle but wasn't sure. Then I heard it again and hiked back to our camp area to see what was up. When I got there, Tala told me that the sound had come from farther down the road."

At this point I took up the narrative, explaining that I went after Jacob but never caught up with him. I told it all, from the time I hurried down the highway, my encounter with the roadblock of the fallen Jeffrey pine, the frightening experience of stumbling upon a rattlesnake in the tree, getting to the Monte Cristo Campground and learning that Jacob had never made it there, to hiking back up to our campsite with a helicopter circling overhead.

Holly, more than ever resembling a cat - - motionless, with her eyes half closed, seeming aloof - - suddenly pounced on me like a feline on its prey.

She pointed an accusing finger in my direction and said, "You should have gone with him to begin with and may have prevented his death."

Tala shot back, "Or they both could've ended up dead!"

Yon gave his account next and said, "After Jacob left, I couldn't stand being idle while Mikey was so sick and needed help. I figured that there was a slight chance the forest rangers got through to their station by then. So I hiked up along the creek. It was no use. When I got to the Mill Creek Summit Forest Service Station, there was no one there, and I hiked back down, taking the road this time."

Marcelo asked, "Did you come across Curtis on the way down?"

"No, I saw nobody."

Todd took up the tale. "When hearing the whistle call, I thought that either Jacob, James, or even Curtis blew it and any of them could be in danger. I decided to check it out and asked Marcelo to come with me."

I said, "You didn't want to go alone because of wild animals?"

"That never entered my mind." He gave an embarrassed chuckle and admitted, "I didn't want him hanging with Candie."

He continued, "We first hiked along the stream. Marcelo walked to the right of it, and I trekked parallel to the creek on its left. The terrain was rugged and I kept a good lookout but didn't see anyone. Then I found an easy spot to jump over the creek and met up with Marcelo, and we cut across to the highway and went as far as Candie's car. Again, there was no soul around.

"The tree blocking the road was massive and looked extremely hard to cross over. Going around it would have been even more treacherous. We thought that someone might be stuck in it and yelled out the names Jacob, James, and Curtis, one after another, but got no response. We got close to a rattlesnake and it began to rattle its tail aggressively, freaking Marcelo out. I wasn't comfortable either; there might have been more rattlers crawling around in the branches of that tree. So we hiked back up to the campsite."

"I guess it's my turn," Candie said. "After Marcelo and Todd left, I got real antsy too and went down the ravine where Jacob had tossed my smartphone. I took Nicklaus with me, and we thoroughly searched the sizable area. It was extremely steep, and I had to slide down on my fanny."

Holly asked, "Who is Nicklaus?"

"He's my intelligent poodle. Anyhow, we rummaged through bushes, and hunted amid all sorts of debris, but had to finally give it up. By the way, I did spot part of a tent, half buried between rubble, but my phone was lost forever. I'll admit, at the time I was really pissed at Jacob. The phone certainly would have come in handy and could have saved us. There was no way I'd have made it back up the steep cliff, so we hiked down to the creek and cut back over to the campsite from that side."

Hannah said, "London and I made up our minds to go check out the damage from the rockslide on the road. Anything was better than to sit around and wait. We had gone a short distance beyond Mill Creek Summit when we heard a helicopter and turned around."

And she looked directly at Marcelo and stated, "We did not see Curtis either, nor anyone else, on the highway."

When no one volunteered further comments, Marcelo said, "We know that Min, Tala, and Mikey stayed in the car, so that leaves you, Derek."

Derek shrugged and said, "I don't have much to tell. After everyone left in one direction or another, I started to have a twinge of conscience. Was I too rough on Curtis? I couldn't even tell where in the face I'd punched him. Must have a black eye by now, I thought. Part of the reason I came on the camping trip was to get closer to my bro. Now I'd really messed up. So I went looking for him.

"First, I searched the area down by the creek but couldn't find him. I did see Candie and her dog near the cliff, though. Then I traversed over to the highway, and again there was no sign of Curtis. I was gonna head down toward Monte Cristo but changed my mind and hiked up the highway, thinking Curtis had headed back to the campsite. Once there, I didn't see him hanging out. I peeked inside the van, but he wasn't there."

Marcelo asked, "Did you talk to anyone at the campsite?"

"There was nobody there."

"How about in the cars? Did you see anyone inside?"

"The van was empty. I saw Min and Tala when glancing into the SUV's window but didn't stop to talk to them."

"But you heard the whistle?"

"Nope, didn't hear it," Derek replied.

Then he continued, "By that time, I started to wonder where the hell Curtis could have taken off to. So I went down to the creek again and from there hiked up toward Mill Creek Summit. I hadn't quite reached the summit when I heard the helicopter. Thank God, I thought, we're being rescued. So I turned around and hightailed back to camp."

There was complete quiet in the room, and it was obvious that we were all reflecting on that day in April which proved to be Jacob's last.

Holly suddenly broke the silence and blurted, "So except for Tala, Min, and the boy, nobody has an alibi for that crucial time."

Everyone seemed shocked at her blunt statement. Then Todd said, "But none of us had a motive. Murdering a guy for being pissed off at getting us into a tight spot is a bit farfetched, don't you think?"

Marcelo said, "Precisely! Even if someone in our group would be this crazy, James also organized the trip, so the murderer would have had to kill him too. And do not forget, we all agreed to the no gadgets term before coming on the trip."

Holly commented, "Of course there has to be a better motive. We just don't know it yet."

Candie put in her two cents' worth and said, "I'm sure if the police dig deep enough, they'll come up with motives. Even I have a good idea of one person's motive."

Curtis gave her a hostile stare and said, "Don't just hint at stuff. Get it out in the open. Which person and what motive?"

She said, "Sweetie, I don't want to embarrass the person in front of everyone, so I won't give a name, but I did overhear a heated argument at the creek. It ended with the person I have in mind yelling at Jacob, 'I won't let it rest; I'm going to make you suffer for it!'"

CHAPTER 30

On the drive home Holly remarked, "The Kims are a lovely family. And what an incredible voice coming out of Min. She touched me deeply with her gospel song."

"You were not alone," Tala agreed.

After a pause Holly stated, "I don't believe for a moment that Jacob accidentally fell off that cliff. He was an experienced hiker and mountain climber. Now that I've met everyone in the group and listened to each person's story, I'm more convinced than ever that this was foul play."

Tala said, "I've got to hand it to you, Holly. It took guts to confront them with the alibi and motive question."

Holly continued, "People's accounts of their movements after Jacob headed down the hill on foot was interesting. And dismissing the idea of a stranger having attacked him, it is obvious that one person, possibly even two, lied to us. I need to know what happened to Jacob before I can go on with my life. In fact, I'm planning to do a background check on each person. It may lead me to a motive. Thanks to the internet, background research is relatively easy nowadays."

I said, "Do you think that's wise?"

"What do you mean?"

"Let's say you discover a motive and confront the person with it. If you've hit upon the killer, you've put your own safety at risk."

"Oh, I won't do that. I'll go straight to the police with my information."

"All I can say is, be extremely careful!"

A minute later Holly said, "I get the feeling that most people were being jerks to Jacob on that trip and can't understand why. For crying out loud, you guys financed the whole thing! I'd have expected some appreciation. Were they being nasty to you too?"

"Not that I'd noticed," I replied. "We were all on edge during the windstorm, and being trapped scared the shit out of us. Jacob took command and I guess came across as domineering to some." And after a pause I remarked, "Come to think of it, he was domineering from the very beginning."

After we had dropped Holly off at her residence, Tala said, "I wish she'd leave the sleuthing to Lieutenant Yager."

"That makes two of us!"

And she asked, "What do you make of Candie's hint?"

"I don't know what to think of it," I replied. "Regardless of whether there is any merit to her allegation, she's playing a dangerous game."

"Think she made it up?"

"I doubt that. Most likely she did eavesdrop on someone's conversation with Jacob and is now fishing for that person to take the bait. If she wanted an explanation of the words she overheard, she'd have mentioned a name."

"I thought she didn't name the person in order not to embarrass him or her."

"That's what she said, but I don't think she withheld the name out of kindness. Calling people 'Sweetie' isn't fooling anyone."

"What are you saying?"

"She may have blackmail in mind."

Tala did not comment, and we drove the rest of the way home in silence.

Once in bed and turning off the light, she said, "I hope you're wrong about Candie."

"Me too," I replied.

CHAPTER 31

Nearly a month had passed since our gathering at the Kims, and I had forgotten about Holly's plan of doing background checks on the group. Preoccupied with other matters, I had in fact been able to put Jacob's death, if not completely, at least partially out of my mind. The deadline to hand in my manuscript was coming up in December and I still had a long way to go. The daily pressure of getting lots of writing done was eating at me. And there was another issue. Despite our best efforts, Tala had not become pregnant. After extensive examination and tests, her gynecologist gave her a thumbs up prognosis. Now it was my turn to get tested, and frankly, I'd chickened out and had not even made an appointment.

On Sunday, late afternoon, November 10, Tala brought up the subject once more and said, "Have you made an appointment with the doctor?"

"Not yet," I admitted. "Focusing on meeting my deadline of December 13 made me forget to call. The way it's going, I doubt I can have the manuscript ready by then." And with a half-hearted attempt at humor I added, "The 13th falls on a Friday; I should have realized from the start that I was out of luck!"

"Speaking of your book, did you ever figure out what to do about the jewelry display case?"

"I couldn't make my original idea work, so I ended up changing the plot and made the villain out to be the jewelry dealer. That meant I had to revise and change dialogue and description throughout, even entire chapters."

She smiled and said, "But you're making it all fit and work out in the end, like you always do. Right?"

"Sure, but it was, and still is, time consuming. No wonder I'm behind schedule and in a rat race against time."

"Can't wait to read the story!"

"I doubt it's your kind of book," I said.

"All your books are 'my kind'."

I grinned and said, "That's what I like about you; you stand by your man!"

We ended the discussion with my promise to call the doctor's office first thing Monday morning, when Holly showed up at our doorstep.

CHAPTER 32

Holly greeted us with, "Okay, I came up with possible motives."

We got her settled in the den, and she said, "With the help of the internet and Jacob's belongings, I made some progress. Thank God he was a saver, never getting rid of things. Some of the stuff I found in his computer files dated back to high school days. So far, I couldn't bring myself to discard anything of Jacob's, haven't even gone through his clothing. And I'm really glad that he told me where he kept his passwords. I found a list of all the campers' first and last names, and he'd shared where he knew each person from before he went on the trip. So that part of the research was easy."

She opened the "Notes" application on her iPad, saying, "Let me read you my list of the suspects' possible motives." And grinning, she added, "Since I know you so well, I didn't do a background check on you guys."

"Thanks!" Tala remarked.

She started reading from her notes, "Yon and Kim: No criminal record. They both emigrated from South Korea, he as an adult and she with her parents. She went to high school and college here, majoring in music. Both apparently lead impeccable lives; I could not find a motive for either one. That doesn't necessarily mean that there aren't any.

"Candie: No criminal record. Had a minor confrontation with the paparazzi, a couple of speeding tickets, two marriages and divorces. Vowed revenge in high school when Jacob ditched her for a red-headed Jock of a girl."

Before she could go on to the next person, I asked, "How did you figure that out?"

"Since I knew that they went to high school together, I studied Jacob's senior yearbook. Candie Leutenegger - - her name before she changed it - - was one of the senior prom princesses in Queen Jessica Johnson's court. Surprisingly, there were only two pictures of her in the entire yearbook; her class picture and the princess one. Jacob's pictures, on the other hand, were all over it. He was prominent on the football and basketball teams, and also part of the student body.

"But I digress. I looked through the students' handwritten comments in the yearbook. Some were typical teenage chatter, others dramatic, and many well wishes for a bright future. Anyway, among all the scribbles, I found one from Candie and it read, *'Jacob, I'm holding no more grudge about you ditching me for the redhead Jock. Honestly! But there is no accounting for bad taste. Have a good life. Candie L.'"*

I said, "That silly comment in the yearbook is hardly cause for a motive!"

"No, but I followed up on it by checking the senior pictures for redheads. It wasn't hard to find the Jock among them. She was prominent on many other pages, excelling in girls basketball, volleyball, and gymnastics."

She laughed and continued, "I told you that Jacob kept everything. I found a list of people he hung out with at his 10-year reunion. Among them was the redhead under her married name. I gave the woman a call and she volunteered the information. According to her, Candie had dated Jacob and naturally expected him to ask her to the senior prom. Days before the dance, they got into a fight and he asked the redhead instead. Candie made a scene and shouted that she would get even with him. My source couldn't remember Candie's exact words, overheard by a crowd of students, but they amounted to something like, 'You double-crossing SOB. I'll get my revenge, even if it takes years!'"

Holly continued reading from her notes, "Todd: No criminal record, but Jacob took him to court in a dispute about a botched roofing job. Jacob won the suit. It was a matter of $10,000, plus Todd had to come up with his and Jacob's attorney fees, which I'd guess added up to double that amount.

"Hannah: No criminal record. Is a gay rights activist." She looked up from her iPad and remarked, "Jacob was not homophobic, so there's no motive there. Actually, I could not find a motive for Hannah.

"London: No criminal record. Seems to lead a flawless life. She did briefly cross paths with Jacob, though. He joined a debate team in college and excelled at it. He was on a debating competition tournament for UCLA, and his team made the finalists, where he faced London as his opponent from Berkley."

Tala interrupted and said, "How on earth did you stumble on that bit of news?"

Holly replied, "Jacob was one of these rare guys who kept meticulous records of anything going on in his life, big or small. All I had to do is type each name of the camping group people into his document file search engine to find the files. You, James, were in his 'Jury' file. I even came across a journal he kept about me. It was dated over four years ago and started with, 'Today, I met this awesome woman named Holly,' but I'm off the subject again.

"Getting back to London and your question, Jacob had written a piece on all his college debate team events. The arguments between UCLA and Berkley - - or rather, between Jacob and London - - got pretty heated. In the end, the judges awarded the win to UCLA, which, according to Jacob's notes, pissed off the Berkley team.

"Derek: Has a record. Was charged for assault when having a confrontation with a disgruntled pawn shop customer. The charges were later dropped and the matter settled out of court. Several speeding tickets on a motorcycle. As per a Sierra Mountaineering Club member, Derek was in a dispute with Jacob when together on a North Shore Lake Tahoe climbing excursion."

"What did they fight about?"

"The person I talked to wasn't sure but thought it had to do with Derek not following Jacob's instructions. Jacob was the experienced rope climber and gave orders on technique. The way I understood it, Derek wasn't paying attention and later goofed off, putting the other climbers in jeopardy. According to the club member, Derek was short tempered and had many run-ins with Jacob during that Tahoe trip.

"Curtis: Also has a record. Was arrested in bar brawls. Has two DUI arrests. He is a racist; known to make slurs about African-Americans and Asians, but most of all, has anti-Semitic tendencies."

Holly looked up from her notes and said, "You know, of course, that Jacob was Jewish."

I said, "Don't tell me you learned about Curtis being a racist from Jacob's files!"

"Certainly not. I put a little effort into that research. I first went to the brothers' pawn shop and bought a small collectable item, making sure someone other than Derek or Curtis helped me. I pretended to be interested in the younger brother and asked the employee where Curtis usually hung out. He gave me the names of a couple of bars. The first had a woman bartender who was not cooperative, but behind the second bar counter worked a cute guy who was susceptible to my flirtation. He gave me all the goods on Curtis I asked for."

Holly closed the iPad and said, "That leaves Marcelo. At first, I wasn't able to find any information about him. When I punched his name into Jacob's document search engine, all I got was last April's camping list. I also could not get a public record of him and guessed it had something to do with his being from Chile. I put him out of my mind and tackled everyone else first. Then, last week, I suddenly thought, Chile, of course! Jacob mentioned that by coincidence Marcelo came from the same small town that he stayed at during his trip in Chile.

"I found the Chile journal in Jacob's 'travel' document folder. There were several pages about his rock climbing experience in the Chilean Andes, but I won't go into that. Jacob roomed with a Chilean family whose oldest daughter was 15 years old. The girl was infatuated and seriously pursued Jacob, but he knew better than to get involved with a minor. When he rejected her, she got mad and told her family that he had made passes at her. Her father threw him out, forcing him to find other digs in town."

She sighed and continued, "I was going to let it go. After all, it had nothing to do with Marcelo. Then I thought, no, I owe it to Jacob's memory to make things right. This happened five years ago, before I even knew Jacob. The girl would now be a woman of 20. Maybe she had a bad conscience all these years and would be eager to tell the truth. I was able to give the international operator name and address, and sure enough, the family still lives there and I obtained their phone number.

"I pulled myself together, practiced what I was going to say in Spanish, and made the call. I asked for the girl by name but was apparently talking to her mother, who said she was married and had moved away. I mentioned that Jacob died and that I would like to set something straight. Even though my Spanish isn't the greatest and she didn't volunteer any English, she seemed to understand. I hadn't even finished explaining when she said, 'I am sorry Jacob died, but so glad to hear from you. Our daughter told us only two years ago that she lied and that Jacob did nothing wrong. We didn't know how to get in touch with him, and now it is too late for her to apologize.'

"The woman was really nice, and just before we hung up, it occurred to me that she may know Marcelo, since he was from the same small town. So I asked, and, guess what? Marcelo is the woman's nephew. In other words, Marcelo and the girl are cousins!"

"It's a small world after all," Tala joked.

And I asked, "So what are you hinting at? You see a motive in all that for Marcelo to kill Jacob?"

Holly said, "Let's assume that Marcelo heard about the alleged inappropriate passes toward his cousin. South American families are extremely protective of their female youngsters. He's a junior in college now, so he's probably a little older than his cousin. He may have vowed revenge for the girl. According to her mother, she only came clean two years ago, and by that time Marcelo was already a student here in California. Imagine the shock he may have had when talking with Jacob at Jock Master Sporting Goods and realizing this was the American that made advances to his cousin."

She cleared her throat and went on, "The way I figure it, Marcelo would be smart enough to keep his cool so that Jacob had no idea that he was related to the girl. Then later, Marcelo may have joined the camping group for the sole purpose of seeking revenge."

We kept silent for a long moment. My head was spinning from paying keen attention to Holly's monologue. I had to digest all the information and suggestions she had brought to the table.

I finally said, "You've done impressive research! I'll keep some of your techniques in mind when plotting my next book."

"Are you making fun of me?"

"Not at all," I assured her. "I'm bowled over by your resourcefulness."

Her green eyes searched mine to make sure I was not bullshitting her and then she said, "Thank you!"

Tala checked the time and asked, "How about eating dinner with us? I can have it ready in about an hour."

"Thanks, but I've got a house to show to prospective buyers." She looked at her own watch and stated, "I'm cutting it close as it is. I just wanted to run my findings by you."

I walked her to the door and said, "Are you going to fill Lieutenant Yager in on your discoveries?"

"Not yet," she replied. "I first have to separate the weeds from the crop."

CHAPTER 33

Tala was already busy in the kitchen when I returned.

I asked, "What are we having?"

"Pork adobo. The pork belly is already marinated. All I have to do is cook it."

"Yum, I love your Filipino dishes! Can I help?"

"You can make the rice a bit later. Right now, just keep me company."

I pulled up a stool to the center island and watched as she heated the metal pot with a little oil, tossed in the marinated pork belly cut into chunks, and sautéed for a few minutes. Then she added water, whole pepper corn, and dried bay leaves, bringing it to a boil.

Lowering the flame, she said, "Now I'll let it simmer for about 40 minutes and then add the vinegar and let it cook for another 10 to 15."

She looked me in the eye and remarked, "Holly is putting a lot of time and effort into her search. I hope it doesn't interfere with her job."

"Real estate agents schedule their own hours, so I don't think time is a problem. I worry more about her safety," I replied.

"I wish she'd let the professionals do the sleuthing, but I can understand her motivation. She thinks that she owes it to Jacob."

She gave the adobo a quick stir and then said, "Amazing what Holly discovered! I'm still trying to take it all in. Who would have thought that many people in the group had cause for a grudge against Jacob?"

And after a moment's reflection she asked, "Do you think we should let the lieutenant know about what Candie hinted at?"

"You mean what she claimed to have overheard at the creek?"

Tala nodded.

"If we had more to go on, I'd say yes, but we don't know which person she alluded to, and I don't even remember her exact words."

"Guess you're right. That's not enough to bother the police with. Speaking of Candie, she called and specifically asked to speak to you. Sorry, I forgot to tell you."

"When was that?"

"A few days ago, it slipped my mind."

"I'm sure it's not important. Most likely she's going to bug me about the movie part again. The woman must be desperate. As far as I know, she hasn't landed a major role in a long time. I'll call her back tomorrow."

"Right after your call to the doctor!" Tala managed to throw in.

Later, as we sat down to a scrumptious dinner of tossed salad, pork adobo, and rice, we savored every bite and tried to forget about Jacob's fate, Holly's sleuthing, and Candie's allegation.

CHAPTER 34

On Wednesday morning, November 13, I was logging on to the L.A. Times website to get my daily news and stared at the headline. It read, *"Candie Valentina found strangled to death at Hansen Dam Lake."* Even now, over eight years later, I still remember the sensation of little hairs standing up at the back of my neck.

After the initial shock, I read on and learned that a Lake View Terrace resident had stumbled on Candie's strangled body while walking his dog at Hansen Dam Lake in the late afternoon of Tuesday, November 12. The news article explained that the location where she was found was not the Hansen Dam Lake's recreation center or fishing pond, but rather the isolated area of the old lake's riparian basin. It went on to question what prompted the actress to venture into the secluded spot and whether she went there of her own free will or was murdered somewhere else and then dumped in that area. The news brief ended with the information that the Los Angeles County Sheriff's Department was in charge of the homicide investigation.

I reread the words once more, making sure I'd gotten it right, and then hurried to our bedroom. On her days off, Tala tended to sleep in. She was stirring, though, and I told her the appalling news. She mumbled something incomprehensible, turned to her other side, and promptly went back to sleep. So much for shock value, I thought.

She finally showed up for breakfast and said, "I had the most disturbing dream. In it you told me that Candie was murdered."

"That was real," I said. "I read it in the online paper."

"Oh God! This is awful. First Jacob and now Candie. Are the two crimes connected?"

"There is a good chance that they are, unless some demented kook or a stalker attacked her."

"This is really awful," she repeated and stormed out of the kitchen.

A short time later, I heard her take a shower. Who could blame her for having lost all appetite? If I hadn't eaten my breakfast beforehand, I doubt that I could have sat down to it now. In anticipation of getting a lot of writing done, I had risen early. Now the knowledge of the dreadful discovery at Hansen Dam had robbed me of any creative thought.

I still sat at the kitchen center island staring into space when Tala, dressed with purse in hand, brushed by me on her way to the front door.

"Where are you going?" I asked.

"Saint Anthony's, to pray for Candie's soul and the soul of her killer," she replied.

I heard the door bang shut and thought, do I deserve such a good woman?

CHAPTER 35

The phone rang all day long. Every person that had been part of our camping trip, and even others, wanted to talk about Candie's murder. The alarmed outbursts ranged from, "How horrible!" "Poor woman! Who would do such an atrocious thing?" to, "Are we all in danger?" "There is a murderer among us. Who is next?" Fear and panic took over, and although worried myself, I tried my best to ease their minds.

I repeated the same words to each caller, "Let's not jump to conclusions. Candie's murder may have nothing to do with Jacob's death and could have been committed by one of her Hollywood connections or a stranger. There could be a crackpot out there with a celebrity obsession. Until more is known about the crime, there is no reason to get spooked."

I had expected to hear from Holly, but there was no word from her, and I became uneasy. By early evening, I couldn't take the suspense any longer and called her.

After four rings, the answering machine kicked in and I was about to hang up and try her cellphone, when I heard a breathless "Hello!"

"Holly?"

"Of course it's Holly, who else? What's up, James?"

"Thank God you picked up. You had me worried."

"Why?"

"Haven't you heard the news?" I asked, perplexed.

"I've been on the go all day showing houses and just walked in the door. What's going on?"

When learning the bad news she did not utter a word, but I heard her take in her breath.

I was wondering if she was still on the line when she commented, "So her spiel about overhearing an incriminating conversation between Jacob and someone was actually true. I thought she'd made it up in an attempt to either throw suspicion on somebody else or make herself important. I really didn't see this coming."

I tried to put forward my stranger theory, but she wasn't buying it and said, "Come on, James. Don't act dumb!"

"What do you have in mind?"

"It stands to reason that she was blackmailing someone."

"You may be right."

Then she said, "Candie was my main suspect, so I have to regroup my ideas."

"Have you taken your findings to the authorities?"

"Not yet. I need to narrow down my hunt and single out the right person before I can give them the information."

"No, Holly! It's too dangerous. Look what happened to Candie. Do it now."

She changed the subject and asked, "How is Tala dealing with it?"

I replied, "She prays."

Holly didn't respond.

Again I urged, "Go to the police with your information."

"Don't worry, I will," she assured me.

"Now!" I said and hung up.

CHAPTER 36

After dinner, I didn't feel like talking to anyone, not even Tala. I told her that I'd go for a ride because I needed some alone time.

She understood and said, "And I'll curl up with a good book, and if more people call, I won't bother to pick up."

I drove aimlessly around the neighborhood at first, then hopped on the nearest freeway. Subconsciously, I exited at a familiar off-ramp and came to a halt by the sports bar where Jacob and I used to hang out. I had not been here since the day that he and I made the damn bet which had set the fatal events in motion. What possessed me to end up here now, I had no idea. Must be an urge to come to the source in order to put it all behind me, I rationalized.

I hesitated for a moment, then parked and entered the establishment. A fair amount of people were eating dinner, seated at the many tables clustered about the place. I went straight to the bar and ordered a beer. Then I glanced at the big screen TVs scattered throughout the room, showing a variety of extreme sports in action, anything from scuba diving in Hawaii to snowboarding at North Island, New Zealand.

The bartender sat a beer in front of me, and I settled on watching an NBA basketball game on the screen immediately above the bar. The Lakers were playing the Nuggets at an away game at the Pepsi Center in Denver.

I was absorbed in the game when the TV set suddenly went blank and a news brief about Candie appeared. Shit, I thought, there is no escape from the horror. An eye witness was being interviewed, saying that he saw the actress's Mercedes parked at the Hansen Dam parking area on the afternoon of the previous day. When asked how he knew it was her car, he stated that he'd noticed the personalized license plate "Candie" when jogging by. At the time, he hadn't known that the car belonged to the movie star Candie Valentina, but after hearing the news of her strangulation, he remembered seeing the car.

When the game continued on the big screen, the patrons seated at the bar had lost interest in the Lakers and Nuggets, the general discussion gravitating to Candie and her fate.

One guy said, "That eliminates her being killed somewhere else and then dumped at Hansen Dam."

Another commented, "So what was she doing there?"

"Obviously meeting someone in secret," the former said.

"You think one of her ex-husbands had something to do with it? I heard that her last one – his name escapes me right now – had a temper and was possessive of her."

"Anything's possible."

The talk then turned to the movies they'd seen Candie in: some great and memorable, others mediocre. They agreed that she may not have been the most terrific actress that ever lived but gave her a 10 in the looks department.

A guy sitting two seats over from me said, "Word is out that she was involved in that other death."

"What other death?" asked the person to my right.

"Remember the body they found at Crystal Lake?"

"Oh yeah, the man who went missing during a camping trip."

"Yep, that one," said the first guy. "Candie Valentina was one of the campers."

"Get out of here!"

"It's true. I have it from a reliable source."

The guy sitting next to me said, "Think the two crimes are related?"

"I wouldn't be surprised," said the other. Addressing me, he asked, "What do you think?"

I shrugged and said, "I just came here to have a beer," promptly paid for it, and got up.

Before I was out of earshot, I heard one say to the other, "The dude that just left looks familiar. Do you know who he is?"

I was too far away to catch the answer.

CHAPTER 37

On Friday of the same week, Lieutenant Yager came around for another interview. This time he showed up alone. I told him that Tala was at work. No matter, he said; he'd catch her later and chat with me first. I was not fooled by his choice of words. Even without his underling, this was an official visit and not an idle gab.

He said, "Now then, Mr. Eaton, no doubt you've heard of Ms. Valentina's homicide."

"Who hasn't?" I replied.

"I have to ask all concerned of their movements at the crucial time. Where were you on Tuesday, November 12, from noon until 3:30 in the afternoon?"

"I was home working on my current manuscript the entire afternoon on Tuesday, mainly doing research on the Web, and also managed to write a chapter."

"I take it that you were alone?"

"Correct." And I asked, "When you said just now, 'all concerned,' did you mean the people who went camping in April?"

He gave me a smirk and said, "Yes, that group and other folks in Ms. Valentina's life. At this point it is best to keep an open mind."

He cleared his throat and said, "Let's get back to my questioning."

He pulled a small notepad out of his pocket and stated, "You made a phone call to Ms. Valentina on Monday morning, November 11, at 9:15 a.m. What was that about?"

"I returned her call. I wasn't home when she called the previous week."

"And?"

"One of my books is made into a movie and she wanted me to pitch her for the lead part to the powers that be."

"Did you?"

I asked, "Have you read my book, *Stifle Her Scream*?"

"I don't read mysteries. I like to get away from crime when not on the job."

"Makes sense. Anyhow, she wasn't right for the part."

"I see."

I said, "Unlike me, my wife has a solid alibi for Tuesday. She was at work in the hospital all day."

He grinned again and said, "I'm sure she was, but it still needs to be verified."

"May I ask you a question about Candie's murder?"

"Sure, but I can't guarantee that I'll answer it."

"Was she raped?"

He took a couple of seconds before he replied, "There is no harm in telling you since that information has already been leaked to the media. There was no evidence of rape."

I sighed and said, "Does that mean that her killing is connected to Jacob's demise?"

"We're looking into that."

I held my hands in front of him, palms up.

He stared at me, failing to understand.

I said, "The article in the paper about Candie's murder stipulated that she was strangled. I assume you want to check the size and shape of our hands and fingers."

There was an amused expression on his face when he stated, "Ms. Valentina was strangled with her own scarf."

"Oh, I shouldn't make assumptions." I tried to picture the strangulation and then said, "Nick wasn't with her?"

"Who is Nick?" Lieutenant Yager wanted to know.

"Nicklaus was Candie's poodle."

"No, the only dog concerned was the one owned by the man who found the victim."

"By the way, did Jacob's girlfriend, Holly, contact you?"

"Yes, she did. Yesterday, as a matter of fact. She said that you scared her into coming forward. I wish that people would leave amateur sleuthing alone. They expose themselves to unnecessary dangers. I told the lady as much."

"What do you make of her discoveries?"

"Some of the facts she mentioned were no news to us, and others we're looking into." And he added, "It is interesting that she found a link between Jacob Barrstein and most of the camping group."

"I was intrigued by that too."

He looked me in the eye and continued, "What about you, Mr. Eaton? During our previous interview I learned that you and Mr. Barrstein were old friends, but I don't think it ever came up how you met."

"I got to know him when we were both called to serve on a jury nine years ago."

He nodded and said, "It is not uncommon for people to form lasting friendships that way." Then he asked, "What about Ms. Valentina? Did you know her prior to the camping trip?"

I replied, "I knew *of* her and had seen her on the screen, but we never met in person before the trip."

He gave me a knowing glance and then said, "Tell me what Ms. Valentina implied on the occasion of your gathering at Mr. and Mrs. Kim's house."

"So Holly told you about that."

"Actually, someone else mentioned it, but I'd like to hear your version."

I said, "Candie alleged that she knew a person's motive for killing Jacob. When one of us, I believe it was Curtis, asked her to give us the actual motive and a name, she refused. She did, however, intimate having overheard a hostile conversation between Jacob and that person. She didn't tell us everything she'd heard, only that the exchange of words ended with the person threatening Jacob."

"In what way?"

"I don't remember her exact words. Something about making him pay."

"She used the words 'making him pay'?"

"Or maybe it was 'making him suffer', I really don't remember."

The lieutenant scratched his chin and inquired, "What did you make of Ms. Valentina's allegation?"

"At the time I didn't know if she could be taken seriously or not. I didn't think she made up the whole thing, but felt that she exaggerated the dispute she'd overheard. After all, she was an actress, accustomed to dramatizing events. I discussed Candie's remark with my wife, and the idea of blackmail briefly came to mind. Later, I dismissed the notion. Nobody in our group is rich, so what would be the purpose?"

"And now?"

"Excuse me?"

"What do you think of Ms. Valentina's claim now?"

I reluctantly admitted, "Now it looks like she really knew something and was silenced."

"So you've come to that conclusion," he said, and got up to leave.

I said, "Wait, I have a question about Jacob."

"I'm listening."

"Does your mountain lion theory still stand?"

"If you mean, was his corpse dragged to the Crystal Lake area by a mountain lion, the answer is yes."

"No, that's not what I meant. I'd like to know if he was mauled and killed by the animal."

"There is absolutely no evidence to substantiate that. According to the coroner, the fall down the cliff is what most likely killed him. Whether he accidentally fell off or was pushed remains to be resolved."

"That makes me feel better," I stated.

He peered at me for a second and then said, "Yes, getting mauled by a wildcat is not a pleasant way to go."

CHAPTER 38

Candie's service was held at Forest Lawn in the Hollywood Hills, on Thursday, November 21. I hate funerals. Left up to me, we would not have attended hers, but Tala insisted that we pay our last respects. The chapel filled fast to capacity. The place was so crowded that people stood along the sides and even in the center aisle, with the portal left open to accommodate hordes of fans who gathered at the rear of the chapel all the way out to the forecourt.

There were flowers everywhere: big arrangements at the front of the chapel; smaller ones along the walls of the side aisles; flower chains draped over the ends of the pews; and bouquets, arrangements, and vases with cut flowers all over the court outside.

Tala and I sat in one of the rear pews so that I had a good overview of the folks assembled. Besides the fans, there was the Hollywood crowd with some of the actors who had starred in movies with Candie. Her agent was there, and so was one of her ex-husbands. Someone had pointed out her parents and younger brother to us, mentioning that they lived in Arizona. As far as I could tell, our campers were represented in full force.

At the left-front corner of the chapel, a harpist stroked the strings of her pedal harp in a subdued, strangely soothing tune. When her piece came to an end, a man, whom I presumed to be a pastor, stepped up to the podium and addressed us with a eulogy. He touched on all aspects of Candie's life, starting with her modest childhood and upbringing in Southern California, all the way to her last major role in a film two years ago. He ended with, "There is an old saying which holds true to this day: The good die young."

When the man stepped down, there was complete silence for a couple of seconds, and then someone took his place and shared a memorable moment in Candie's and his life. Spontaneously, others followed suit, contributing experiences, either notable or funny, about the late actress.

As a total surprise, Marcelo took the platform and went into a long spiel of how he had had a crush on Candie ever since his teens when he saw her in a movie shown at a theater in his Chilean hometown. His dark eyes lit up as he told of being blown away when meeting her in the flesh on our camping trip. "The real Candie Valentina surpassed all my expectations!" he said, and described her enthusiasm and good sportsmanship while hiking on the Pacific Crest trail to Pacifico Mountain, despite suffering from blisters on her feet.

Even all these years later, I remember thinking at the time, is this guy for real? Has he forgotten what a pain in the ass the woman was to Jacob and the rest of the group?

There followed more anecdotes of praise from members of the congregation. Then   Candie's favorite hymn was announced and played - - I can't recall the name of it - - and the ordeal was finally over.

Getting out of the chapel was a slow process. I tried not to stumble over loved ones and fans. Once out in the open fresh air, I was more than ready to leave, but Tala pulled at my elbow, saying, "I'd like to say a few words to her parents."

Trying to fight the crowd on our way over to Mr. and Mrs. Leutenegger, Candie's agent blocked my way and said, "Well, hello there, Mr. Eaton! Sorry you couldn't recommend Candie for the lead in the movie adaption of your book." And with a smug smirk he continued, "Not that it matters any longer."

I had never met the man before, but my dislike was instantaneous. I said a few meaningless words, and then he spotted someone important in the entertainment business and took off.

When we finally squeezed and shoved our way over to Mr. and Mrs. Leutenegger, we found the middle-aged pair dazed. Candie's mother was leaning heavily on her son's arm. I was under the impression that their daughter's death, especially the circumstances of it, failed to have sunk in yet. We introduced ourselves, and then Tala found the right words of comfort and I just stood there, nodding. We were about to make a retreat when Yon and Min came to pay their respects.

Min offered, "Our family would be more than happy to give Nicklaus a good home."

Mr. Leutenegger replied, "Thank you, but Candie's agent took the dog, as Nicklaus is already used to him." And he addressed the four of us and said, "You're all invited to an informal lunch at the Beverly Wilshire."

I turned around, prepared to get away at last, and made eye contact with Lieutenant Yager. Is he a fan or here on official business, I wondered.

CHAPTER 39

I was going to skip the luncheon, but Tala had other plans for us. She was full of enthusiasm, having never been to the posh Beverly Wilshire before. I had not seen the inside of the place either, but could have spared myself the pleasure with ease. As I remember the gathering, *informal* is not the word I would have used.

They had rented a hotel ballroom, and it was set up with large round tables, accommodating about a dozen guests each. A substantial flower arrangement adorned the center of every table. My horticultural vocabulary is limited; all I recall is a bunch of white and purple flowers.

The room started to fill as we got there, and it seemed natural that all campers settled around the same table. To my surprise, Holly joined us.

I asked, "What are you doing here?"

"Candie's parents invited me."

"That's not what I meant. Why did you come to the funeral? As far as I know, you only met

Candie the other night at the Kims' house. And don't tell me that you're a big fan; I won't buy it."

"You're right on both accounts."

"Again, why are you here?"

She smiled sweetly and said, "Let's just say I have an interest."

I gave her an intense stare and then said, "Yes, I get it."

Some in our group could not help but whisper to one another and glance frequently over to a table where prominent entertainment people sat. Even Tala, my down-to-earth woman, was in awe of the celebrities. A waiter came around and asked for our preference; the choice was either a meat or fish dish. I went with the meat. I can't say off hand what it was, only that I liked it.

The Kims were sitting next to Tala and me, and Min said, "Mikey is going to be disappointed. We told him that we might be able to adopt Nicklaus."

I said, "I'm positive Nick would have liked living with you better than with Candie's agent."

Derek, seated all the way across from me, said loud enough for all to hear, "I wonder who's paying for this big shindig!"

Hannah, who took it as a direct question, replied, "I'd assume her parents, or else the money may come out of Candie's estate."

"I doubt it," Derek prompted. "She was in financial trouble."

"And how would you know that?" the former asked.

"She came to hawk a diamond necklace, ring, and bracelet set a couple of weeks before she was killed."

We gawked in astonishment. Then Holly said, "That makes you the last person of the group to see her before she died. My guess is that no one else did since the get-together at Yon and Min's house."

London volunteered, "Actually, she wanted me to ghostwrite a story she was going to tell about our camping experience. I went to her house for a preliminary discussion."

Marcelo said, "To my great surprise, she was kind enough to let me treat her to dinner."

Todd admitted meekly, "I took her out too."

Curtis blurted, "Anything for a free meal!"

Todd shot him an angry glance, and Marcelo said, "Shame on you!"

As if on command, everyone suddenly was preoccupied with eating their lunch. In the lull between the main course and dessert, I excused myself and went in search of the men's room. When I came back, the conversing at our table was divided into one-on-one chats, with about five different topics being discussed. I didn't want to butt in on any of them and frankly was not interested, so I just sat, letting my mind drift.

I was thinking, wouldn't it be nice to get out of here, drive home, fix myself a warm beverage, sit at the center island in our kitchen, open my laptop, and get lost in my manuscript? The next best thing was to record and store it all in my head, and type my thoughts into the computer later.

I was rudely pulled out of my creativity as Derek suddenly got out of his chair, walked over to my side of the table, and patting me on the shoulder, said, "Sorry, dude, for you having been dragged here, what with your funeral hang-up and all. Sorry about your mother, too."

Tala was busy discussing the merits of physical therapy versus surgery with Hannah, so I could not even engage her in a dirty look, but I was fuming inside. There was no excuse for her blabbing my problem to the group.

To Derek I managed to say, "That's okay," and was relieved when he went back to his spot.

When after dessert and coffee Mr. Leutenegger stood up and thanked everyone for coming, the occasion had officially come to an end. I was glad to leave, at long last.

CHAPTER 40

As soon as the valet had brought my car and Tala and I were on our way home, I said, "Do you realize how angry I am with you?"

"What did I do?"

"Don't give me that! You had no right to discuss my mother! I resent it."

"What are you talking about? Your mother didn't come up in any conversation I'm aware of."

I told her about Derek's remark.

"Oh that! When you went to the bathroom, they wanted to know why you seemed so upset. Someone, I think it was London, said you must really mourn Candie more than the rest of us. So I explained that you've had a problem with funerals ever since your mom died and that I had to practically force you to come."

"And that's all you said?"

"Of course. What else did you think I said?"

"Never mind. You're forgiven," I replied. "Let's not talk or think about funerals anymore."

When we exited the freeway and got close to our neighborhood Tala remarked, "Funny how Candie stayed in some people's lives."

"Yeah, that was a surprise. The bombshell about her being so broke that she resorted to pawning her jewelry is almost comical."

"Don't make fun of the situation, James. I think it's sad. I'm wondering why she was in financial difficulties."

"A good guess is that she lived beyond her means in the last two years, while out of any major jobs." I chuckled and added, "She was resourceful, I give her that. Since I wouldn't recommend her for the part in *Stifle Her Scream,* she came up with the idea to write a book about our camping disaster. She was also clever enough to admit to herself that she was no author and meant to hire London as ghostwriter. I think it would have worked. She had a story to tell, and given her name and popularity, she had a good chance to land a major advance from a big publishing house."

We were turning into our street when I commented, "I'd like to know what Candie wanted from Marcelo and Todd, besides a free meal like Curtis intimated."

Tala said, "What makes you think she had alternate motives? Couldn't she just have enjoyed going out to dinner with them?"

"Don't be naïve. Marcelo is a brain, and may even be considered cute by women, but he's basically a kid, and a poor student from Chile at that. Todd might be tagged a good-looking stud, but he's a roofer. In other words, a blue-collar guy. Broke or not, *the* Candie Valentina does not go out on dates with guys like them."

Tala brought up a different matter and said, "Thanksgiving is coming up next week. My sister and family are still vacationing in the Philippines, so we're on our own. Let's invite Holly. She has nowhere to go."

"Fine by me," I said.

CHAPTER 41

The smallest turkey Tala could find was 11 pounds, but none of us had a problem with leftovers. We had mentioned to Holly that bringing a friend would be welcomed, but she showed up alone.

When the bird was out of the oven and needed to sit for a while, I was setting the table with our good china and opened the bottle of chardonnay Holly had brought, as the two women put the finishing touches to mashed potatoes, green beans and gravy.

For the first time in our lives we sat down to a Thanksgiving feast with only three people on Thursday, at 4:30 in the afternoon, November 28, eight years ago.

During the meal Holly said, "This holiday sure is different, but the turkey is done to perfection, and I'm enjoying the trimmings too, not to mention the good company. Thanks for having me."

Without any prompting she continued, "I could've gone to Albuquerque, where my folks live, but I wasn't up for being smothered with sympathy. Don't get me wrong, I love her dearly, but Mom tends to get over dramatic. "

"Is that where you usually spend Thanksgiving?" Tala asked.

"No, we flew to Florida and celebrated with Jacob's parents for the last four years. They always had a slew of people over who were so much fun."

A single tear rolled down her cheek, and she wiped it away in an annoyed motion and said, "How about you? Where is your favorite Thanksgiving hangout?"

Tala replied, "My sister and I take turns, but she's in the Philippines at the moment. My brother-in-law comes from a huge family, so we're used to being a crowd. Today is different for us too."

Holly said, "Your parents also live in the Philippines, right?"

"Yes, my entire clan does, except for my sister, who's also married to an American and lives here, the one who went home to visit now."

Holly looked at me and said, "I know that your mom passed away, but you've never talked about your dad. Did he also die?"

"I wouldn't know. According to Mother, he was a nuisance and embarrassment. She divorced him when I was four. He and I never stayed in contact, and I only have a vague memory of him."

Tala said, "Besides being a bit of a playboy, the man was a fortune hunter. That's why James's mother threw him out. She was the one with the big bucks."

No doubt, Holly had noticed the forbidding glance I'd cast at my wife and changed the subject. She asked, "How long have you been married now?"

"11 years."

"You also never told me how you two met."

I laughed and said, "I have to thank my acute appendix attack for getting us together! She was the nurse who tended to my physical and emotional needs after surgery. It was love at first sight for me. Tala, however, needed a bit of persuading."

Tala said, "He happened to be engaged to another woman at the time, and I had scruples." And she continued, "You met Jacob online, correct?"

"Yeah, we hooked up with the aid of a Web dating service. They matched us perfectly, I think."

The expression on her face turned to sadness, and it was obvious that we had touched on an open wound.

After having finished eating the main course, I said, "I'm stuffed. We'd better serve the pies later." And turning to our guest, I remarked, "If you'd have brought a friend along, we could play cards. It doesn't work with a threesome."

"I can't get my life back and befriend anyone until Jacob's death is solved. I thought you understood that."

"Oh, I didn't specifically mean a man. You could have invited any friend - - woman, guy, whoever."

Tala said, "I'm not in the mood to play cards anyway. Let's just talk."

And so the conversation drifted to the memorial service of the week before and consequently to Jacob's and Candie's deaths. With Holly present, the discussion could not have gone any other way.

She first said, "What we learned from the pawn shop brothers, London, Marcelo and Todd is suggestive."

"You mean that she was in financial trouble?" Tala asked.

"Yes, but more important that several people of your camping group met with her a few days before she was killed."

Tala countered, "Doesn't it make sense that these meetings were harmless, since the individuals freely admitted to seeing her?"

I said, "They must have known that it eventually would come out anyhow and thought it looked better if they mentioned seeing her right off the bat. The police have a way of checking up on these facts. Lieutenant Yager already obtained Candie's phone records, so he knew about my phone call to her."

"What phone call?" Holly wanted to know. So I had to explain it to her.

"That's wonderful news about your book being adapted into a movie. Congratulations!"

Then she went on, "I might have to dig a bit, but the fact that Candie was eliminated is an indication that she knew something about Jacob's death. For instance, do you remember the exact words she used at the Kims when hinting at a conversation she claimed to have overheard between Jacob and that other person?"

I said, "As you may recall, Candie didn't tell us what that alleged heated exchange of words was all about. She only stated the last sentence thrown at Jacob by her mystery person. The wording she used went something like this, 'I won't let it go; I'm going to make you pay for it!'"

Tala corrected, "I think it was 'I won't let it rest.' And she may have also said 'I'm going to make you suffer for it,' not 'pay'."

"That sounds like what I remember her saying too," Holly agreed.

I asked, "What did you mean by you may have to dig a bit?"

"Remember all the stuff I learned and told you about after doing a background check on each person?"

"More or less."

"Well, I'm planning to interview them one by one and hope I can corner the guilty person when bringing up their past. There has to be a link to what Candie overheard and the suspect's background."

She sighed and admitted, "As hard as it is for me, I'll concentrate on Jacob's death for now and deal with Candie's murder later."

Before I could protest and remind her again of the danger involved in her plan, she continued, "I'm also going to have each person go over the events of your camping trip, day by day. I'm counting on the concept that someone remembers something useful."

She looked us in the eyes and stated, "I'll start with you two!"

CHAPTER 42

For dessert Tala served traditional apple and pumpkin pies with coffee, and I brought a bottle of Kirsch, which German friends had given us as a gift, to the table.

I remarked, "In Europe they drink this as a digestive, I'm told. Appropriate after our heavy meal, don't you think?"

The ladies poured a small amount of the liquor into their coffees, and I drank mine from the shot glass. Unlike the cherry brandy, Kirsch is not sweet, but has a subtle flavor of cherry and a bitter-almond taste. It burns as it goes down.

Swallowing her last bite of pie, Holly queried, "So tell me about the camping trip. What did you do each day and evening?"

I said, "As you well know, the trip was cut short, so it is only a matter of two-and-a-half days, before disaster hit on Wednesday."

"Yes, I'm aware of that. So tell me already."

"When we got there on Monday, we pitched our tents and got settled. Right off the bat, Jacob caught Candie using her smart phone and tossed it down the cliff, but you already know that. Then Jacob gave us his rules, which sounded bossy of him but was necessary. He fixed us prime rib for the first dinner, and while we roasted marshmallows on the campfire, he had us introduce ourselves. After that, we discussed April Fools and other pranks."

"What kind of pranks?" Holly asked.

"Practical jokes that people pulled. Some dating back to their childhoods."

"Whose idea was it to talk about pranks?"

"Jacob suggested it. He was basically in charge of all activities."

"Tell me about the pranks."

"I forgot most of them. I really wasn't in the mood for childish antics."

Tala took over and said, "I remember the stories, some are funny." And so she retold what she had retained of everyone's tale. I was surprised at her good memory. She ended with my made-up contribution.

Holly listened carefully to each person's episode and commented as Tala went along. About Jacob's prank she said, "That surprises me. Jacob was such a law-abiding citizen as a rule. His friend must have coerced him to do it."

About Hannah's math class she recalled, "We did something similar once in my English Lit period." And she giggled when Tala told Marcelo's altar wine story and remarked, "I can just picture the priest, spitting out the vinegar in front of the congregation!"

Of Candie's auditioning anecdote she stated, "That was no harmless prank but a self-serving deception." And Holly roared with laughter when hearing Todd's skinny-dipping antic, and grinned when she pictured Tala's home-economics teacher trying to get into her sewed up jacket sleeve.

After listening to my silly bed-peeing tall tale, she said, "And you made that all up on the spur of the moment?"

"Like I said, I wasn't in the mood, or I'd have come up with a better story," I replied.

"More coffee?" Tala asked our guest.

"No thanks, I'm full to the brim. But please go on with your account of the camping trip."

I continued, "Next morning, Tuesday, April 2, we tended to personal hygiene. It was early when I went down to the creek. I came across Marcelo, who was carrying water up to the campsite to do dishes, and I talked to Jacob by the stream. After breakfast, we got ready to go on a long hike to Pacifico Mountain."

I was starting to describe the hike when Tala interrupted and said, "Maybe we should tell Holly about Jacob's fit when he realized that Candie was gone."

Holly said, "Candie left? I wasn't aware of that!"

"She didn't actually quit the camping trip. She just drove to the Monte Cristo Campground and bummed a shower from a family in their motorhome. She came back a short time later."

"Clever of her," Holly commented.

"Yeah, but Jacob was furious when her car was gone and he thought she'd left for good, assuming he'd already lost our bet."

I rendered a brief description of the hike along the Pacific Crest trail, explaining that the Kim family turned back about three miles after Mill Creek Summit. I mentioned Candie's blister and Curtis's run-in with Jacob about smoking pot. I also mentioned Candie's attempt to pump me about getting the lead part in the film, which would eventually be made from my book, while we ate our picnic lunch at Pacifico Mountain.

Then I described the bocce ball game we played once back at our campsite. I emphasized that the wind started to pick up already before dinner, so that we could not have a campfire, but gathered by the big tent after the meal. I stated that Jacob made us sing empty-headed songs, and that the highlight of the evening was when Min treated us to a solo from Carmen. And I pointed out that Mikey was already getting sick at that time, so the Kim family had turned in early.

Holly remarked, "Min tugged at my heartstrings with her gospel song. Now you tell me that she also sings opera. What a talent!"

My narrative continued with the information that the windstorm got severe and woke us up at two o'clock Wednesday morning, with our tents blowing away and all of us seeking shelter in the cars. I said that by dawn it became clear that Mikey was severely ill and needed medical attention. Without going into details, I conveyed the panic and general discord among us when finding that we were trapped between the fallen Jeffrey pine on the road below and the boulders caused by the rockslide above, near Mill Creek Summit.

I ended with, "Jacob decided to hike down to the Monte Cristo Campground to get help, and you already know the rest, in particular what we all did after he left."

Holly nodded and said, "Yes, when getting together at Yon and Min's, we learned of people's whereabouts during Jacob's task. And it was clear to me then, and is still clear to me now, that with the exception of Tala, Min, and the boy, all had opportunity to kill Jacob. And since that is obviously not getting me anywhere, I'm concentrating on motive."

I said, "I don't see how telling you the events of the camping adventure in chronological order helped with motive."

"I can't see it either, yet. I'll go home and think about it. And don't forget, you are only the first two people I've interviewed. Maybe some of the others can give me useful info."

"I wish you'd leave it alone and let the lieutenant handle the investigation. It's just too dangerous for a layperson."

Holly didn't seem to have heard my last sentence. She stared into space, deep in thought. Tala got up and cleared the dessert china away.

I followed my own train of thought and nearly jumped as Holly, all of a sudden, burst out, "What was Candie doing up there to begin with? I mean, camping is not the kind of activity one associates with the likes of Candie Valentina."

Tala, coming back from the kitchen, remarked, "She admitted to Jacob after he caught her trying to send a text to her agent that she made the trip in the hope of a publicity stunt. And since we now know that she had money problems and was out of work, getting noticed by the press and being labelled a star who could 'rough it,' may have gotten the attention of a producer or two."

"That's a possibility."

After a long pause Holly said, "How about if she made the trip for the sole reason to meet you, James?"

"That's absurd!"

"Not really. She was desperate for the lead role in the movie adaption of your book. She didn't want to corner you out of the blue, but befriending you casually on a trip and launching her approach must have seemed like a great idea to her."

She eyed me keenly and asked, "Did she flirt with you?"

"Not that I noticed."

Tala stated, "Sure she did!"

"When was that?"

"Up at Pacifico Mountain, just before she pinned you down about the movie deal."

I shrugged and tried not to smile.

Holly said, "That settles it. Candie obviously thought she could charm her way into getting the part."

Then she suddenly seemed in a rush to leave. I wondered whether she was anxious to go home and write down all she'd learned.

She remarked, "I had better get going. I'm taking the day off tomorrow but plan to get up at the crack of dawn to take advantage of Black Friday."

Tala said, "I work the early shift and also need to be up before daylight." And turning to me, she added, "And you have a doctor's appointment."

"Don't rub it in!" I said.

Holly thanked us, happily accepted some leftover turkey to take home, and was gone.

While we cleaned up the kitchen and stacked the dishes in the dishwasher, I said, "Holly is determined to play detective. I fear for her safety."

"Me too, but she is driven, there's no holding her back. In a way, I understand where she's coming from. If it would be you who got killed, I'd feel the same way."

We were already in bed when I asked, "What if the tests show that I have an infertility problem?"

"Then we'll find out what our options are and go from there." And already half asleep, she mumbled, "Don't worry. You'll be fine."

CHAPTER 43

I stayed awake for a long time, not sure if the heavy meal, two glasses of wine, and the shot of Kirsch were to blame. Or maybe the reason for my restlessness was deep rooted somewhere in my brain. In any event, the conversation with Holly replayed over and over in my mind. When I escaped into a fitful sleep at last, I suffered a nightmare where someone chased me with a butcher knife. I woke up, hearing myself scream, "Don't cut me! I'm not infertile!"

Tala held my hand and said, "You had a dream. Go back to sleep. You'll be fine. I'll reset the alarm clock to 7:30 for you."

She kissed me on the forehead, and a minute later I heard our front door bang close, knowing it must be 5:00 a.m. and she was on her way to the hospital.

I never heard the alarm, and it was 8:30 when I woke again. My appointment was at 9:30, and the doctor's office was only a 15-minute drive away. I could easily make it, I thought, and decided to eat breakfast first. Then I hustled into the shower, got dressed, shaved, and was brushing my teeth when I heard the doorbell ring. Go away, whoever you are, I thought.

I had just finished spitting out the mouthwash when the bell rang again. Shit, this better be important, I thought, and shouted, "Coming!"

When opening the front door, I found Lieutenant Yager and Deputy Sheriff Knox standing at my threshold.

I said, "Oh, did you make progress in your investigation?" And not waiting for an answer, I added, "This is not a good time. I have an appointment."

The lieutenant assured me, "I won't take long."

I looked at my watch and said, "Come on in, then."

As soon as they were inside my home, he got formal and stated, "Mr. James Eaton, you are herewith under arrest for the murders of Jacob Barrstein and Candie Valentina."

"I want to talk with my lawyer," I said.

"You may in due course," Lieutenant Yager replied, "but first things first."

I remained silent when Deputy Sheriff Knox snapped the handcuffs on and read me my Miranda rights, but I knew the race was over. To my great surprise, I felt nothing but tremendous relief.

CHAPTER 44

I won't go into any of the boring booking procedures that followed, nor the jail time before the trial, not even the trial itself. But I do need to address how I was nailed for the crimes, and go into details of the murders.

On November 29, the morning of my arrest, I had a vague idea that Holly had figured it all out, but was taken aback as to how fast she apparently had contacted the authorities. Not only that, it seemed impossible to me that she had been able to convince them that her suspicions were correct. After all, law enforcement agencies did not arrest people without proper cause. It turned out that what led to my arrest had nothing to do with Holly.

To my astonishment, it was Candie herself who supplied the evidence. The actress was a lot smarter than I had given her credit for. Her agent, having taken over Nicklaus after her death, discovered a SD-card stashed in a small pouch attached to the dog's neckband. It ended up being a video that Candie took of herself. At the time of my arrest, I didn't know of the video's existence, but found out about it much later. The video was presented as evidence and played at my trial. It showed a selfie of Candie and she gave the following testimony:

"My name is Candie Valentina. In case something should happen to me, I am herewith making a statement. I was present at a camping trip, organized by Jacob Barrstein in April of this year. When walking my poodle, Nicklaus, early in the morning on our second camping day, April 2, I overheard a heated argument between Jacob and his friend James Eaton. I wrote this all down so that I would remember it later. Jacob was at the creek when James walked up to him and shouted, 'You miserable SOB! I've tormented myself for ten frickin' years about getting to my mother too late, and it was all your stinking fault!' Jacob said, 'I don't know what the hell you're talking about.' To which James yelled back, 'That idiotic prank you pulled, turning the arrow the wrong way, made me get lost. I was on my way to my mother's deathbed at UCLA Medical Center, but because of you, she died before we got a chance to make peace. I won't let it rest; I'm going to make you suffer for it!'

"I am making this video on Monday evening, November 11. I have a meeting with James Eaton tomorrow at Hansen Dam to enact a role I may possibly play in the film adaption of his book."

So this video of hers was damning to me on both Jacob's and her murder. Never mind that she blackmailed me into giving her the part.

CHAPTER 45

Far from trying to justify my actions, I trust that the reader wants to learn the morbid details. I'll start with Jacob's murder.

When Jacob told his hair-raising prank and the rest of the group found it funny, all hell broke loose inside me. It took every bit of my willpower and restraint not to cuss him out right then and there. During the entire time that others told their tales, I paid no attention and could only think of what Jacob had done to me and how it had affected my emotions for ten years. As he pressured me into telling a prank of my own, I made the peeing story up but could not get Jacob's words off my mind, doubting that my story made any sense.

Finding him alone at the creek the next morning, after he was responsible for another of my sleepless nights, I lashed at him verbally, which gave me some relief. When I threatened him with the words, "I'll make you suffer," I did not know what I had in mind, but certainly not murder.

It initially was an accident; we had a fistfight and he fell down the cliff. In my entire adult life, I had never before resorted to physical confrontations, preferring to fight my battles with words. After elementary school, I had left physical fighting behind me. But I'm getting off the subject. I told my story of how I went in search of Jacob after he left for the Monte Cristo Campground many times before, skipping the essential part. Now I will tell it all.

My previous narrative was accurate, up until I finally emerged out of the Jeffrey pine that had blocked the road. While I took a moment to catch my breath, recovering from the struggle to climb across it, I saw Jacob trekking back up the highway, walking toward me at a fast pace.

Knife at the ready, he said, "I saw a rattler in the tree earlier. Glad to know that you're okay."

Seeing him walk toward me with a knife made me lose my head. I had taken up karate, so kicking it out of his hand came without effort. It flew in a wide circle down the drop-off.

"What the hell did you do that for?" he said. "I heard the whistle and came to check out the situation."

My only reason to go after Jacob had been, as Tala suggested, to make sure he was safe from wild animals. But something snapped in my brain when I saw him walking up the hill, coming at me.

He saw the fury in my eyes and said, "What are you so sore about? You won the bet, what more do you want?"

I shouted, "Who cares about the bet? I thought you were my friend! Laughing your head off and congratulating yourself that you were *home free* with the prank, like you said, never mind that you caused me to make wrong turns and get lost! You think it was all fun and games?"

He calmly said, "So you're still mad about that. Be reasonable. How could I have anticipated that you would drive to the hospital to see your mother? I didn't even know you then!"

That he could be so placid and nonchalant about it made me even angrier. And what he implied next set me off in a tantrum.

He grinned and said, "Be honest, the real reason you are so hung up on your mother is because she cut you out of her will."

I shoved him, he pushed back, and before long we were in a full-blown physical fight. He was two inches taller and in better shape, but I had the karate training and an adrenaline rush working for me, so we were an even match. Without realizing it, we got close to the gorge and Jacob fell down the bluff. I almost joined his fate but held on to the edge for dear life and hoisted myself back up. I will never forget the scream that escaped him as he went flying.

After the scuffle - - which could have easily turned out the other way, with me being the one tossed down - - I honestly wanted to get help and needed to desperately believe that he wasn't hurt bad. That is when I blew the whistle a second time. Then, when continuing my hike down, I started to worry that I would not be believed and accused of wanting to kill him on purpose. I was also more and more certain that he could not have survived a fall down the cliff. Had I been thinking rationally, it would have occurred to me that my deed might have passed as manslaughter, not murder.

By the time I reached the Monte Cristo Campground, I had convinced myself that I'd be booked for murdering my friend if I told the truth. I decided it would be in my best interest to keep quiet about what had happened. And so I pretended to never have caught up with him. Once I played that game, there was no turning back. I had to keep up the lie.

CHAPTER 46

Candie had called me in the spring, soon after Tala and I got back from the disastrous trip, pumping me again about getting the lead role in the *Stifle Her Scream* movie. Then her agent sent me an e-mail on October 11, with a formal request. I did not realize how desperate for the part she was, though. At the Kims house, when Candie first hinted at the confrontation she had overheard between Jacob and me, I ignored it. I had no way of knowing if she even caught more than those last words. I was not convinced yet that she planned blackmail.

Tala had forgotten to mention Candie's call to me until a few days later. She must have called sometime before Sunday, November 10, and I returned the call on Monday, November 11, and sure enough, she suggested meeting with me concerning what she called "a delicate matter." When we met at a Starbucks that same afternoon,

Candie recited the accusation I had shouted at Jacob down by the creek, practically word for word. She threatened to go to the police with her information unless I recommended her for the part. I had expected as much, but when she actually made the blackmailing proposition, I was surprised at the extreme anger that welled up in me.

Outwardly, I kept my cool and said that I would consider it, and all of a sudden she was all over me with "Sweetie this" and "Sweetie that." It was sickening, but I played along. Of course, I had no intention of giving in to her. Blackmailers never stop with the initial demand. I had no idea what she could possibly want from me further, if she got the role, and I had no interest in finding out.

I came prepared, bringing a tablet along and having her read from the electronic edition of my book. I chose the dialogue of the main character, Jamie, from a couple of chapters. She was actually not bad, I have to admit. I pretended to be ready to take her up on her deal.

When we parted I said, "I'd like to see you act before I make the final decision. Remember the low-flying small airplane scene?"

"Definitely."

"I'd like to enact that scene."

"Sure, no problem."

"Let's meet tomorrow afternoon at Hansen Dam Lake. Say, 2:00 in the afternoon. You know where that is?"

"It's in the San Fernando Valley. I've been there once," she said.

"Do you have a bright colored scarf or shawl, preferably a red one?"

"Yeah, sure."

"Bring it along."

"Do I have to wear it?" she asked.

"You don't. We need it for you to wave at the plane, remember?"

"Of course, how stupid of me!"

"Wear appropriate shoes. The terrain is unpaved. And don't bring Nick. I'm going to have you run in the scene; he would be a hindrance."

"Okay."

"That's settled, then," and I gave her directions where to park and which path to take when walking toward the lake.

There was no airplane scene in my book, so she had not even read it. She may have scanned reviews but was ignorant about the story. The nerve of the woman! I was furious at her already for having the balls to blackmail me, but insisting that she was perfect for a part she had no clue about pissed me off even more.

I got there ten minutes early. There were only a few cars in the parking area, Candie's not among them. I did not come across a soul on my walk in the direction of the lake. The place seemed deserted. The parked cars must belong to people who stayed in the adjacent park, I deduced.

The area around the lake was overgrown with trees and bushes. In the distance stretched the imposing 2-mile-long, 97-foot-high flood control dam. I waited for her at the appointed spot in the riparian basin and started to worry that she may bring the dog along anyway. Knowing Candie, she was not one to follow orders. With Nick around, I would have to give up the entire plan.

I sighed with relief when she showed up alone.

She looked in all directions and said, "What beautiful wild scenery! I don't remember the area being so isolated."

"There are always plenty of people walking, jogging, or biking up on the dam, but the region down here is not that well known, although horseback riders are common."

"You come here often?"

"Now and then," I replied. "Let's get started with the scene."

Since she had no idea what my book was about, I made up stuff as I went along. I first explained that this was a scene requiring dialogue and interaction between Jamie, played by her, and Fred the villain, played by me. I told her that Fred was a psychopath and had lured her to this remote spot. But that was all contrived; there was no Fred or psychopath in my book. She was to pretend to like him, even being in mortal danger. Under no circumstances was she to show fear or he would attack her. At one point there would be a small airplane flying overhead, and she would run away from the trees into the open, waving her scarf to get the pilot's attention.

"Did you bring the scarf?" I asked.

"Sure," she said, and reached into her purse, showing it.

"Perfect, a red one! You can put it back in your bag. We won't need it until later."

I then made up dialogue, which we rehearsed. I won't go into all that, but most of the lines were hers, since supposedly I was evaluating her acting. I corrected her a couple of times, and made her do them over.

I finally praised her and said, "Okay, you've got your lines down pat. Now, at the end of your last line, we both look up toward the dam, pretending we hear an airplane. Then you pull the scarf out of the purse and run into the open, waving it violently, as you see the make-believe plane flying overhead."

"Got it," she said.

"Okay, let's do the entire scene, starting from the beginning."

So we did. And when she ran, waving the scarf in the air, I said, "No, no, not like that! Come back, I'll show you."

Once she was back at our spot, hidden from sight by trees, I told her to face the direction of the dam so that I stood directly behind her. Then I grabbed the scarf away from her saying, "You hold it like this" - - and in one swift motion, I wrapped it around her neck and pulled tight.

She struggled a little, but it was over in no time, and I let her drop to the ground. I made sure that she was not breathing, without touching her. I took a quick peek around, listening for footsteps. The coast was clear; there was not a soul in sight. Then I strolled back to where my car was parked and drove off.

If someone on horseback, a jogger, or bike rider would have passed by while we practiced dialogue, no harm done, but I would have had to abandon my plan to strangle her. The actual strangulation was over and done with so fast, that I felt it was worth the gamble.

Looking back, I can see how clever, and at the same time how dumb, Candie was. Shooting that video of herself and stashing it in Nick's collar bordered on genius. She may have even planned to destroy it if I came through, but I doubt it. That video was to be her permanent hold over me. But meeting with me in an isolated area, even in broad daylight, was pure stupidity.

EPILOGUE

At the beginning of this book, I had served eight years out of my life sentence, and now that I come to the completion of the story, I've served nine. The incarceration has given me plenty of time to think about my crime and punishment, and I deserve what was dealt to me.

During the trial, my lawyers claimed that I was demented from years of self-accusation about my mother's death and tried to plead insanity. That might have been the case with Jacob. Ten years of mental suffering plus the anxiety of being trapped on the mountain may have pushed me over the edge. Yet, I was as sane as the next guy when killing Candie. In any event, the jury wasn't buying it.

There is something else I need to address. In the course of Lieutenant Yager's second interview with me, he mentioned that the fall down the cliff had killed Jacob but never explained the details. From the coroner's testimony at my trial, I learned that Jacob had broken his neck and with a 99% accuracy it was determined that he died immediately after the fall. That made me feel a tad better, knowing that he didn't linger and suffer. But one part of the investigation puzzled me at the time, having to do with Jacob's body.

If he was killed instantaneously and could not have moved away, why did the helicopter pilot fail to spot his body? I saw the chopper circle and hover over the area for a long time when trekking back up the hill. And if a mountain lion allegedly carried Jacob's corpse off, why didn't the pilot, or me, for that matter, witness it?

Now, having had many years to reflect on it, I came to the conclusion that there could have only been two possibilities. Number one, although the cliff consisted of mostly rock formation, there were a few small shrubs visible here and there, and Jacob was wearing khaki pants and a bone-colored top. If he was partly hidden by a shrub and his clothing blended in with the rock face, there was a chance that the helicopter pilot missed seeing him.

And number two, which is far more likely, the wildcat was right on the spot during Jacob's fall and carried him away before I even got down to the Monte Cristo Campground, or hiked back up along the creek, and certainly way before the chopper got on the scene.

As far as telling the story goes, I have an incredible memory, so recalling events accurately, years later, was not a problem. Being precise about dates and times, however, turned out to be a tedious research chore.

I was treating this real life work like I would any of my fictional mystery novels by not revealing the identity of the murderer until the end. By the same token, I wove subtle clues and red herrings throughout. A couple of passages in particular come to mind. Who would have thought that "having a word or two" with Jacob at the creek was in reference to a full blown verbal accusation? And in the very first chapter, I make the statement, "My psychiatrist tells me that I need to write about the event in order to get closure." What reader would come to the conclusion that I was talking about the prison shrink? As for closure, I doubt that I will ever have it. My daily routine here is a constant reminder of my crime.

Prison life is harsh, and I have to be on my guard against the hardcore inmates. Yet, I doubt that I would be comfortable on the outside. Technology has become so advanced in the last eight years – and there is no stop to it – that I would never catch up. I read about new discoveries and scientific breakthroughs and keep up with current events, but it is not the same as experiencing it firsthand.

I have an inkling that Tala suspected me but was in denial. I don't think that she initially associated Jacob's prank with my getting lost on the way to Mother's deathbed, but after the killings, she may have connected the dots. She never questioned me, but her subtle little mannerisms gave her away. On the day the news about Candie's murder came out, the way Tala looked at me when she said she'd pray for Candie's soul and the soul of her killer made me wonder how much she knew and how much she guessed.

Tala did come visit me on a regular basis for the first couple of years, but I knew it would not last. And who could blame her? She is now married to someone else and the proud mother of two kids.

Needless to mention that I missed my doctor's appointment on the day of my arrest and never learned if I am indeed infertile. At this point in time, I don't give a damn.

Stand-Alone Mystery by Alice Zogg
A Bet Turned Deadly

R. A. Huber Mysteries by Alice Zogg

Guilty or Not
Murder at the Cubbyhole
Revamp Camp
Final Stop Albuquerque
The Fall of Optimum House
The Lonesome Autocrat
Tracking Backward
Turn the Joker Around
Reaching Checkmate

Available at www.amazon.com,
www.barnesandnoble.com
and other vendors.